"Jessica, I don't think I've ever seen you look so beautiful," Zach Marsden said softly, staring deep into her eyes. It was Wednesday afternoon, and Jessica and Zach were sharing a picnic on the quad. Zach's gaze was so intense that Jessica's heart caught in her throat. "Your eyes are the same color as the sky," he whispered. Then he buried his face in his hands, groaning. "I can't believe I just said that."

Jessica laughed, relieved that the tension was broken, and then she sunk her teeth hungrily into a hunk of soft bread. Zach was so thoughtful. He had prepared an elaborate picnic of French bread, Brie cheese, red grapes, and cold pasta salad.

At first, being with Zach had just been fun, but now she was starting to have serious feelings for him. She knew she should tell him the truth about her age. And about Ken. She had almost summoned the courage the night before, but then she had stopped herself. He would never forgive her if he knew she had been lying to him.

If there's one thing I hate, Jessica thought glumly, *it's guilt.*

JESSICA'S
OLDER GUY

Written by
Kate William

Created by
FRANCINE PASCAL

BANTAM BOOKS
NEW YORK · TORONTO · LONDON · SYDNEY · AUCKLAND

RL 6, age 12 and up

JESSICA'S OLDER GUY
A Bantam Book / November 1995

Sweet Valley High® *is a registered trademark of Francine Pascal*
Conceived by Francine Pascal
Produced by Daniel Weiss Associates, Inc.
33 West 17th Street
New York, NY 10011
Cover art by Bruce Emmett

ISBN: 0-553-56637-7

Published simultaneously in the United States and Canada

Bantam Books are published by Bantam Books, a division of Bantam Doubleday Dell Publishing Group, Inc. Its trademark, consisting of the words "Bantam Books" and the portrayal of a rooster, is Registered in U.S. Patent and Trademark Office and in other countries. Marca Registrada. Bantam Books, 1540 Broadway, New York, New York 10036.

PRINTED IN THE UNITED STATES OF AMERICA

OPM   0 9 8 7 6 5 4 3 2 1

To Jordan David Adler

Chapter 1

"Uh, no . . . nothing's wrong," sixteen-year-old Jessica Wakefield stammered. Nervously, she reached for her water glass and accidentally knocked it over. She lunged for the glass but missed, and water splashed all over the floor. Jessica took a deep breath and folded her hands together, giving her date, Zachary Marsden, a weak smile.

Zach bent down under the booth and retrieved the glass, watching her with concern. "Jessica, are you *sure* you're OK?"

It was Tuesday night, and Jessica and Zach were at a popular diner near Sweet Valley University. The diner was old and dingy, with peeling orange walls and cracked vinyl seats. Students had crammed themselves into the garish green booths, and seventies rock music blared out of an old jukebox in the corner. According to Zach, the diner was always packed, particularly in the wee hours of the morning.

1

Jessica and her twin sister, Elizabeth, were in the middle of a weeklong visit to the off-campus apartment of their brother, Steven, and his girlfriend, Billie Winkler, who were both students at SVU. Jessica had met Zach at a party she had thrown in her brother's apartment on the first night of their stay. Zach was a good-looking college junior with sandy-blond hair and beautiful emerald-green eyes. He was a little more conservative than the guys Jessica usually dated—his hair was cut a bit too short, and he tended to wear preppy clothes. But he was gorgeous, charming, and genuinely nice. And most important, he respected her intelligence, which was a relief after her recent debacle with the SATs.

Since Jessica had been at SVU, she and Zach had gone out every night—to a hip vegetable-juice bar, to the campus coffee bar, to a cozy little restaurant in the mountains, and now to this diner. Zach had even treated her to a moonlight tour of the campus. So far everything had been perfect. Except for the small fact that Zach had no idea she was only in high school. He had just assumed she was a college student, and at first she hadn't found any good reason to let him know the truth. But now the lie was becoming too difficult for even Jessica to maintain.

To make matters worse, Jessica wasn't the only one interested in Zach. Magda Helperin, the treasurer of Theta Alpha Theta, the most exclusive sorority at Sweet Valley University, was after Zach, too. A striking sophomore with fair skin, jet-black hair, and crystal-blue eyes, Magda was one of the most popular and influential girls in the sorority. She would be even more important in two years when Jessica started college—and pledged Theta Alpha Theta.

Jessica had been prerushing the Thetas all week, establishing a name for herself for her future at SVU. But ever since she had learned of Magda's interest in Zach, Jessica had lived in constant fear that she and Zach would be discovered together. If Magda told Zach the truth—and she would, if she found out that Jessica and Zach had been dating—Zach would never speak to Jessica again, and Jessica would be banished from Theta Alpha Theta forever.

Jessica had planned to tell Zach how old she really was, to get that part of the problem out of the way, but she had waited too long. Now it looked as if Jessica's worst fears were being realized. Magda and a group of Thetas stood in the doorway of the restaurant, waiting to be seated. Jessica was trapped.

"I think my nerves are a little frazzled tonight," Jessica explained to Zach, who was staring at her worriedly. "Maybe I'll order some herbal tea." She grabbed a menu off the next table and held it in front of her face, pretending to scan the selections.

"Jessica, your menu's upside down," Zach pointed out.

"Oops!" Jessica exclaimed brightly, flipping the menu over. "No wonder I couldn't read anything." *Maybe Magda and the Thetas will leave,* she thought hopefully. After all, the diner was pretty crowded. She lowered the menu an inch and peered over the top. No such luck. The group still stood impatiently

3

in the doorway. Magda began to argue with the host. She was flipping her glossy black hair and gesticulating wildly.

"So what did you decide on?" Zach asked.

Jessica lowered the menu reluctantly. "Oh, they don't really have what I want," she said, shrinking down in her seat as unobtrusively as possible. Jessica bit her lip as Magda and the Thetas started threading their way through the crowd, following the host. It looked as if they were heading for a booth right near Jessica and Zach.

"Jessica," Zach pleaded, "please tell me what's wrong. You're making me nervous."

"Nothing," Jessica hissed. Then she added softly, "I'm sorry, but it's nothing. Really." She gave Zach the most reassuring smile she could muster under the circumstances. "I was just trying to get the waiter's attention." She fidgeted with her spoon nervously.

"Do you need something?" Zach asked.

"Actually, I think I'm ready for the check," Jessica said, digging her spoon into her chocolate milk shake and letting her hair fall in a blond curtain over her face.

"But we just got here," Zach protested, indicating the untouched cheeseburger and fries on her plate. "You haven't finished your food yet."

Zach was right. They had just got to the diner. And now, Jessica thought with a twinge of panic, they had to get *out* of the diner—fast. With a surreptitious glance, Jessica saw Magda and her friends take their seats in a corner booth. *Maybe I'll say I'm sick,*

4

Jessica thought desperately. But then she immediately rejected the idea. If she faked an illness to get Zach to take her home, they would have to walk right by the Thetas. She had to find a way to sneak out the back.

Jessica thought fast and summoned up her acting skills. She plastered a worried expression on her face—which, at the moment, wasn't too much of a stretch—and sniffed the air. "Do you smell that?" she asked.

Zach peered at her quizzically. "Smell what?"

"I think . . ." Jessica began, glancing around the diner. "I think I smell smoke!"

"There's a smoking section just behind us," Zach offered.

Jessica shook her head. "That's not what I mean," she said urgently. "I think I smell a fire!"

Zach's eyes grew wide. "I don't smell anything," he told her, looking concerned.

Jessica jumped out of the booth, keeping her face covered with her arm—as if she were trying to prevent smoke inhalation, but really to avoid being seen by Magda. "C'mon!" she whispered to Zach, pulling him out of his seat. "We've got to get out of here!"

"What?" Zach said, a perplexed look on his face.

"There must be a grease fire in the kitchen!" Jessica explained, panic rising in her voice. "Don't you smell it?" She pulled Zach down the hallway toward the back of the restaurant. She looked around wildly for an exit, but the small corridor housed only rest rooms and a phone. "This way!" she called, grabbing his arm and dragging him into the women's room with her.

Now what? Jessica asked herself, glancing around the rest room for a way out. The bathroom was small and dingy, with grayish-pink tile walls, and it smelled strongly of disinfectant. Two sinks stood along the far wall. Jessica bit her lip. She and Zach couldn't hide out in the women's room all night, but they couldn't go back into the diner, either. By this time Magda and her friends would be ordering their food.

"Jessica, I know you wanted to be alone with me, but don't you think this is a little extreme?" Zach teased. He leaned against the wall and tried to pull her toward him.

"Zach, this is no time for jokes," Jessica said, resisting his advances. "The whole restaurant could explode."

"Jessica," Zach asked skeptically, "are you sure you're not overreacting?"

"Didn't you hear the fire alarm?" Jessica asked, a look of pure astonishment on her face. "Didn't you smell the smoke?" She poked her head out the door; the corridor was deserted. "Flames are coming from the kitchen!" she exclaimed, coughing and waving her hand dramatically.

Zach got up and tried to look out as well, but Jessica pulled the door shut firmly. "C'mon, Zach!" she shouted. "We don't have any time to lose!"

Suddenly Jessica noticed a small window near the ceiling on the far wall, above the two sinks. "The window!" she exclaimed.

"Jessica, you've got to be kidding," Zach said, eyeing the window doubtfully. "It's much too high and much too small. There's no way we could get through it."

"Either we get through that window or die trying," Jessica said gravely.

"A pair of star-crossed lovers found burned to death in the women's room." Zach placed his hand over his heart dramatically. "The modern Romeo and Juliet." He grabbed her in his arms. "Quick, Jess, one last kiss."

Jessica tried not to smile. This was the first time she'd seen Zach act so playful. He was more serious than most of the guys she'd dated. In fact, that was what had attracted her to him in the first place. But she liked this side of him. It made him seem younger than a college junior. And she liked the feel of his strong arms around her and the fresh smell of his denim jacket as well. Unfortunately, she didn't have time for a big romantic scene right now.

"Zach, I just don't think you're taking this seriously," Jessica scolded, kissing him quickly on the lips and disentangling herself from his arms. "We've got to get out that window!"

"And just how do you plan on doing that?" Zach demanded.

"Let's see . . ." Jessica began, chewing her lower lip. "I know! It's simple," she said, speaking with more certainty than she felt. "I'll get on your shoulders and open the latch. Then you'll climb up the wall and squeeze out the window. And once you're through, you can reach in and help me out. See? Simple!" Jessica smiled, feeling pleased with herself.

Zach looked stunned. "Did you say you want me to climb up the wall?"

"Sure, why not?" Jessica asked nonchalantly. "You're strong enough, aren't you?"

"Jessica, I study physics and biology," Zach protested. "I'm a premed student, not Spiderman."

"You were also the star player for your soccer team in high school," Jessica reminded him.

Zach sighed. "All right, all right. I give up." He crouched down. "Get on," he instructed.

This will be easy, Jessica thought. *I've done trickier moves with my squad.* She was the cocaptain of the cheerleading squad at Sweet Valley High. She quickly stepped onto Zach's shoulders. He stood up carefully, holding on to her ankles while she reached up to the window and fumbled for the latch.

Jessica grabbed hold of the clasp and turned it. The window sprang open, and a gust of cool air blew into the rest room. "There! I got it," she called, and she jumped off Zach's shoulders gracefully.

"Well, here goes nothing," Zach said, climbing up on the sink. He stretched his body to its full length and grabbed the window ledge with his fingertips. Jessica watched with admiration as he shimmied up the wall, his movements smooth and athletic. Breathing heavily, he balanced on the ledge and grabbed onto the top of the window frame. Holding on to the slender frame for support, he swung his legs through the narrow opening like a gymnast and

8

carefully lowered his body through it, flipping onto his stomach when he was halfway through. Jessica held her breath as she watched him. It looked as if he were going to make it. But then Jessica realized that Zach was struggling. His upper torso had turned out to be wider than the window. Zach growled, squirming and wriggling in an attempt to slip his broad shoulders through the window.

"Jessica," Zach said finally, "I'm stuck." He looked down at her despondently.

Jessica tried not to laugh. With only his upper body jutting into the women's room, Zach looked like a giant panda.

Suddenly a clap of thunder sounded outside. "You're not going to believe this," Zach said, beginning to shiver, "but it just started to rain. Half of me is sticking out a window of a women's room into the pouring rain. I'll never live this down at the fraternity." He moaned and covered his eyes with his hands. "How in the world did I let you talk me into this?"

"Don't worry, Zach. You can fit through," Jessica said encouragingly. "Maybe you should try taking off some of your clothes."

Despite his predicament Zach couldn't help smiling. "You wish," he said. Then he sighed. "But that's really not a bad idea." He wriggled out of his sweater and jean jacket and threw them down to Jessica. Twisting and turning, he managed to squeeze his wide shoulders through the narrow frame. "Jessica," he said before his face disappeared. "You owe me one."

Moments later Zach's head reappeared at the window. "OK, Jess, I've got a footing here on the ivy lattice," he told her, wiping raindrops from his face. "Now, let's get you out." He wriggled his shoulders back through the frame and reached down for her. Balancing on the sink, Jessica stretched her hands up to meet his.

Suddenly tinkling sounds of light laughter and chatter reached her ears, along with the unmistakable smoky voice of Magda. The Thetas were on their way to the bathroom!

"And I saw the most exquisite midnight-blue velvet gown for the formal!" Jessica heard Magda telling the others outside in the hallway.

"Do you think velvet is too wintry for the season?" another female voice replied. Footsteps were rapidly approaching.

Jessica gasped. "Zach, hurry!" she hissed with real panic in her voice. He grasped her by the wrists firmly and lifted her until she reached the window. Jessica squeezed through the narrow space just as the bathroom door opened. Holding on to the window frame with one arm, Zach supported Jessica with the other. She crouched on the ledge and jumped the few feet to the ground, slipping on the wet grass under her feet.

"You OK, Jess?" Zach asked, dropping down to the ground beside her.

"Yeah, I'm fine," she answered. She jumped up quickly and brushed the wet leaves off her jeans. Then she took Zach's hand. "Let's get out of here!" she urged. Jessica could feel her heart pounding in her ears as they ran for Zach's car through heavy sheets of rain.

As they drove away, Jessica took long, deep breaths, trying to calm the beating of her heart. She was dripping wet, from her shoulder-length, tangled blond hair to her black leather pumps.

Zach reached behind him to grab a towel from his gym bag in the backseat. He rubbed it through his hair quickly and handed it to Jessica.

"Thanks," Jessica said with a smile. *Whew, that was a close call,* she thought, toweling off her hair. It wasn't easy juggling Magda and Zach. Or trying to pass herself off as a college freshman. What if Magda had come into the bathroom a few minutes earlier and had caught her in Zach's arms? Or climbing out the window with him? Jessica shuddered at the thought. If she got blackballed by the Thetas now, she would ruin her entire future at SVU. *But I really don't have anything to worry about,* Jessica reassured herself. *I've got everything under control.*

Jessica flipped on the radio to a mellow station and leaned back in the passenger seat, enjoying the sound of the soft music and the steady patter of rain. *SVU is nice even in the rain,* she thought. Then she became vaguely aware of something disturbing her peace. It was Zach, giving her a sidelong glance.

"What is it?" Jessica asked. She unzipped her bag and fumbled through it for a brush.

"Jessica, is there something you're not telling me?" he asked, looking at her suspiciously.

"What do you mean?" she asked, her turquoise

11

eyes wide. *I know I have a brush in here somewhere,* she thought, digging around in the bottom of her purse.

"I mean, why did you want to get out of the restaurant so fast?" he pressed.

"I didn't *want* to get out of the restaurant," Jessica reminded him. She dumped the entire contents of her bag onto her lap and fished through an array of cosmetics. *Aha!* she thought, picking out a small pink brush. "We *had* to get out." She flipped down the window shade and looked in the mirror, combing through her damp hair. *Not bad, considering,* she thought. Her heart-shaped face was flushed a rosy hue from the rain, and her eyes were bright and sparkling.

Suddenly Zach steered onto the shoulder and pulled the car to a halt.

"Zach, what are you doing?" Jessica asked.

"I think we need to talk," he replied, his expression serious.

Oh, no, Jessica thought, *he knows something.* Did he know she was only a high school junior, not a college freshman? That she hadn't transferred from Princeton but was at Sweet Valley University only for a visit with her brother? That Elizabeth wasn't her younger sister but actually her identical twin?

Zach unbuckled his seatbelt and turned around to face her, looking distinctly uncomfortable. A faint flush tinted his handsome face. He reached for her hand and looked her straight in the eyes. "Jessica, you're not dating anyone else, are you?" he asked softly.

Jessica swallowed hard, feeling a sharp twinge of guilt as she thought of Ken Matthews, her handsome, well-built blond boyfriend at home. Ken was the captain and star quarterback of Sweet Valley High's football team, the Gladiators. Jessica and Ken had been a hot item ever since Jessica had gone through a traumatic experience with her ex-fiancé, Jeremy Randall. Did having a boyfriend constitute dating? she wondered. *No,* she decided, *going out with someone is definitely more than dating.*

Jessica tried to look surprised at Zach's question. "What are you talking about?" she asked, forcing a laugh. "You know you're the only guy I'm dating right now."

"Then . . . are you—" Zach hesitated, looking embarrassed. "Are you interested in someone else at SVU?"

No, but somebody else at SVU is interested in you, Jessica thought. She laid a reassuring hand on his arm. "Zach, there is only one guy I'm interested in at SVU," she reassured him. "And that's you."

Zach looked confused. "Then I don't understand," he said. "Why the mad scramble to get out of the restaurant?"

"Zach, I *told* you," Jessica said, a note of exasperation in her voice. "There was a grease fire in the kitchen. I didn't want to go up in flames."

Zach still looked unconvinced. "If there was a fire in the kitchen, then why didn't anyone else follow us out of the restaurant?" he asked, crossing his arms across his chest.

13

Jessica shrugged. "I think most customers went out the side entrance," she said.

Zach raised an eyebrow but didn't pursue the line of questioning further. "OK, OK," he said, raising his hands in the air. "I give up." He turned his eyes back to the road and revved the engine. Jessica heaved a sigh of relief as they pulled back on the glistening road.

"Just one more thing," Zach said.

Jessica groaned inwardly. Why wouldn't he just drop the subject? "Yes?" she asked tightly.

"You owe me a massage," Zach said. He stretched his neck in a wide arc and raised his shoulders. "And I mean a major massage—full back, shoulders, and arms. That climb out the window really cramped me up."

Jessica smiled. "You got it," she said.

"I want to be in fine form for the Zeta dinner on Friday night," Zach said, giving her a rakish grin. "So we can dance the night away." Then he turned his attention back to the road, squinting to see through the torrents of rain. Jessica looked at Zach's handsome profile as he drove, wondering how in the world she was going to manage the Zeta formal with both Zach and Magda there. Zach had asked her to the dinner before Jessica had learned of Magda's interest in Zach. And it was essential that Jessica attend the formal. The Zeta dinner was the most important social event of the year.

Jessica sighed. She had never imagined that life at SVU would be so complicated. After Jessica and Elizabeth took the SATs, the college-entrance exams, Mr. and Mrs. Wakefield had allowed them this weeklong visit to Sweet Valley University to get a feel for college life.

On the first night they had arrived, they had thrown a huge party without Steven and Billie's knowledge. Elizabeth had protested the whole time, but Jessica had managed to talk her into it. The party had been wild, and Steven and Billie's apartment had got trashed in the process. When Jessica had run to save an heirloom vase of Billie's from falling off a shelf, a pair of strong male arms had beaten her to it. Jessica had looked into the greenest eyes she had ever seen. The moment she had met Zach's piercing gaze, she had felt a current of electricity run between them. Zach had just transferred to SVU from an East Coast college, and he had assumed from the start that Jessica was a college student as well.

In Jessica's opinion the party had been a huge success. That is, until the police had come. And until Steven and Billie had found out about it. They had come back from their weekend getaway early and walked into a disaster zone: a keg in the shower, cigarette butts littered on the rug, beer cans everywhere. Steven had thrown a cataclysmic fit, ranting and raving about respect. Elizabeth had just cleaned quietly, that "I told you so" expression written all over her face.

Despite their identical appearances, from their long golden-blond hair to their blue-green eyes to the matching dimples in their left cheeks, Elizabeth's and Jessica's personalities couldn't have been more different. While Jessica, who loved to flirt, had picked up gorgeous Zach Marsden at their party, Elizabeth had befriended shy Ian Cooke, a journalism major who had spent the entire evening with his nose stuck in one of Elizabeth's books. While Jessica had been making friends with the most popular girls on campus, Elizabeth had spoken with hippie, granola types. And while Jessica had been trying to get in good with the Thetas all week, Elizabeth had been blowing off their luncheons to attend journalism seminars and philosophy lectures.

Jessica shook her head. She kept covering for her sister, but if Elizabeth wasn't careful, she would ruin her chances of ever becoming a Theta. But, then, if she herself wasn't careful about the dangerous situation with Magda and Zach, she would never get into Theta Alpha Theta either. Jessica bit her lip as Zach's red convertible Cabriolet sped through the dark university town. She couldn't make any mistakes.

Chapter 2

"You're what?" Jessica gasped, choking on her popcorn and spilling the bowl all over Steven and Billie's lumpy sofa bed later that night. "You're *staying* at Sweet Valley University?"

"Jessica, careful!" Elizabeth scolded. "We're already in hot water with Steven and Billie as it is." She grabbed the oversize wooden bowl and began picking up popcorn kernels off the bed. The weak springs of the secondhand sofa bed creaked in protest as she moved.

"But . . . what . . .?" Jessica sputtered. She glared at her twin. "Explain yourself," she demanded.

Elizabeth decided to make her sister suffer a little. She was still burning from the fact that Jessica had forced her to throw a party behind Steven's back. As usual, Elizabeth had ended up taking some of the flak for Jessica's disastrous exploit.

"You know, because of the party we had Saturday

17

night," Elizabeth explained, pretending to misunderstand her sister's question.

Jessica cut her off with a wave of her hand. "I know, I know," she said, looking exasperated. "I meant, what do you mean, you're staying?"

"Oh," Elizabeth said with a small smile. "*That's* what you meant."

Jessica aimed a throw pillow at her. "Liz!" she said. "Give!"

"OK, OK, I'll explain," Elizabeth said, ducking the pillow. "We've got to shake this comforter out first, though." Jessica groaned but hopped off the bed and helped Elizabeth carry the down comforter to the window. Elizabeth smiled to herself. She had never seen Jessica move so fast to clean up. Elizabeth opened the window, and they shook the blanket out into the windy night.

"Hey, what do you think this is?" an angry voice yelled from below. "A garbage bin?"

"Whoops!" Elizabeth said, stuffing the comforter into her arms and slamming the window shut. She looked at her sister in disbelief. "Jessica," she asked, "is it our destiny to bother Steven's neighbors?"

"Yes," Jessica said, her expression grim. "It is our solemn fate to forever disturb the peace at Steven and Billie's apartment." Both girls giggled.

"Well, I guess we're going to have to finish shaking the comforter out on the rug and then vacuum it up," Elizabeth decided. Jessica ran to get the vacuum cleaner in the pantry. Moments later the comforter was clean and the shaggy burnt-orange rug was spotless.

"Liz," Jessica whined after they had finished, "you're torturing me." She clicked the vacuum cleaner off and put her hands on her hips. "Three days ago you were complaining that a week was too long to be separated from Todd." Todd Wilkins was Elizabeth's longtime boyfriend. "And now you're ready to stay at SVU for good?" Jessica asked. "What's going on?"

Elizabeth thought back. It had all started when she'd met Ian Cooke at the party they'd thrown on Saturday night. Ian was a pale, lanky junior with silver wire-rim glasses and longish brown hair that was constantly falling into his eyes. Elizabeth had found him engrossed in one of her books—a biography of pioneering TV reporter Edward R. Murrow—after the party had broken up. They had started to talk, and they'd discovered that they had a lot in common. Ian had been active on his high-school paper, as Elizabeth was, and they both had ambitions to become journalists. When Ian had learned of Elizabeth's similar interests, he'd invited her to sit in on his advanced journalism seminar with Felicia Newkirk. Professor Newkirk was a world-renowned journalist who had been one of the first female reporters to break into the elite White House press corps.

Elizabeth had been thrilled at the opportunity to attend the seminar. But the minute she'd walked into the class, Professor Newkirk had taken a dislike to her. They'd had an open confrontation in which Elizabeth had defended the merits of TV reporting against print journalism. Professor Newkirk had scoffed, implying that Elizabeth was an inexperienced journalist who would succeed only through her looks. "At least you're pretty," Professor Newkirk had said. "That's all a girl like you will need anyway, especially on TV." Elizabeth still burned at the memory.

Then Professor Newkirk had given the students an unexpected assignment: a one-thousand-word essay on student life, to be written overnight.

"Well, you know that essay I wrote on college drinking for Professor Newkirk's class?" Elizabeth began.

"How could I forget?" Jessica said. "You were up all night typing like a total geek, and you looked like a raccoon for two days afterward with dark circles under your eyes."

Elizabeth decided to ignore her sister's comment. "Well, my essay won the competition, and the prize is an internship at *The Chronicle*, the nationally distributed newspaper."

"Some prize," Jessica sneered. She threw her hands up in the air. "So that's what this is all about. I can't believe it. You're planning to give up your entire life in Sweet Valley for some stupid internship on a college paper."

"Jessica, you don't understand," Elizabeth said patiently. "Professor Newkirk is really important in the field. She could help me get places. And she knows what she's talking about. She thought I should take my high-school-equivalency test, enroll at SVU, and start my career as a reporter."

"Liz, you're only sixteen," Jessica said. "I think Lois Lane must have been at least eighteen when she met Clark Kent."

"Jessica, this is my real life, not *Superman*," Elizabeth said.

"But you're trying to be Superwoman," Jessica retorted.

"Just hear me out, OK?" Elizabeth asked, sitting back against the wall and hugging her knees to her chest. "I've been giving it a lot of thought. And I think Professor Newkirk is right. Journalism is a highly competitive field these days. If I want to be a successful journalist, I need to get an early start in life. I can get my General Equivalency Diploma and enroll at SVU next semester."

"Well, I think the entire idea is ridiculous!" Jessica declared.

"You do?" Elizabeth asked, surprised. She had thought Jessica would turn green with envy when she heard that Elizabeth was going to stay at SVU. "Why?"

"Well, first of all, you're too young," Jessica replied. "You'd never fit in. You'd always be considered an adolescent, and your whole college experience would be ruined because you felt out of place."

Elizabeth pondered that for a moment. "You know, I've thought of that," she said pensively. "But I really feel like I fit in here. I think I'm ready to move on with my life. I mean, sure, it would be hard at times, but I can handle that."

"Well, you may feel you're ready for college, but I doubt Mom and Dad would agree," Jessica put in. "They'd never let you skip your last two years of high school. Just think about it, Liz. It was a big deal for us to miss a week of school."

21

"I'm not so sure," Elizabeth said. "I don't think Mom and Dad will be thrilled, but I doubt they would stand in the way of my higher education. I mean, this internship is such an honor—I should really grab the opportunity."

"What about Todd?" Jessica countered. "I thought you two were going to be together forever."

Elizabeth felt a twinge of anxiety as she thought about her handsome, intelligent, and caring boyfriend at home. She and Todd had always talked about going to college together. An image of Todd's masculine face flashed before her, his deep coffee-colored eyes warm with affection and his smile tender. But then Elizabeth shook off her feelings of uneasiness. Her relationship with Todd had survived worse, and she knew it would last through this separation.

"We *are* going to be together!" Elizabeth insisted. "We just won't get to see each other as much. SVU is only two hours away from Sweet Valley, after all."

"Long-distance relationships never work," Jessica proclaimed.

Elizabeth's eyes widened in surprise. Jessica and Todd couldn't stand each other. In fact, Jessica never stopped telling Elizabeth what a stick-in-the-mud her boyfriend was. She would be the last person in the world to encourage Elizabeth to stay at Sweet Valley High to protect her relationship with Todd. Elizabeth's eyes narrowed. Jessica obviously had an ulterior motive. Elizabeth just wasn't sure what it was.

"Jessica," Elizabeth said carefully, "I'm–surprised

you're being so negative about this internship. I thought you'd be excited for me. I mean, wouldn't you jump at the chance to have some freedom yourself?"

"Well, sure," Jessica admitted. "It would be fun to be on my own and hang out with cute guys and stuff. But . . ." Her voice trailed off.

"But what?" Elizabeth prompted.

"But, Liz, you can't stay!" Jessica protested finally.

"And why not?" Elizabeth asked.

Jessica reached out and grabbed her twin's arm, her eyes filled with sadness. "You can't just abandon your own twin," she said.

"Jessica, I'm not abandoning you," Elizabeth said quietly. "I'm just moving on with my life. We'll still see each other all the time. And talk on the phone."

"But with you gone, Mom and Dad will focus all their worry and attention on me!" Jessica wailed. "I wouldn't be able to get away with anything!"

Elizabeth rolled her eyes. So that was it. "Jessica, our lives are bound to separate sometime," she said firmly. "If you were offered a starring role in Hollywood, would you want me to stand in your way?"

It looked as if Jessica was out of excuses. "Hmmph," she pouted. Then she grabbed a handful of popcorn and munched on it ferociously.

Todd Wilkins let the phone fall with a clatter, his face as white as a sheet. He sat down hard on the couch and dropped his foot, which was encased in a white cast, onto the coffee table with a loud thump. He felt as if he had been punched in the stomach.

It was Tuesday night, and Todd and Ken were in Todd's living room, watching the football game. *I've been spending too much time watching TV since Elizabeth left,* Todd thought despondently. *And now it's only going to get worse.*

"What is it?" Ken asked, pointing the remote control at the TV and turning down the volume.

"It's . . . it's Elizabeth," Todd stammered, running a hand through his curly brown hair.

"Is she all right?" Ken asked with concern. "Is she sick?"

Todd waved his hand dismissively. "She's fine," he said flatly.

"But she's not happy at SVU?" Ken guessed.

"Oh, she's happy," Todd said with a sigh.

"Then what's the problem?" Ken asked, perplexed.

"She's *too* happy," Todd said grumpily. He picked up a throw pillow off the couch and aimed it violently at the TV. "She's not coming back."

Todd felt as if his whole life were falling apart. Recently, at a big basketball game, he had fallen and broken his ankle—in front of all the important college-basketball scouts. He had been wearing a cast ever since. He was out for the season, and his whole athletic future was ruined. And now his present life was a mess, too. His girlfriend was leaving Sweet Valley. Todd sighed and fell back on the couch. *Did I do something awful to deserve this?* Todd wondered.

"She's not coming back!" Ken repeated in shock. "What do you mean, she's not coming back?"

24

"Elizabeth's decided to stay at SVU," Todd explained angrily, whipping his foot off the coffee table and sending a bowl of chips flying in the process. Todd got up and began pacing the room, limping around on his cast. Chips crunched under his feet. "Something about some *stupid* prize for some *stupid* internship for some *stupid* newspaper . . ." He felt as if he were going to burst with rage and frustration. He had been counting the minutes until Elizabeth returned, but no . . .

Todd picked up a basketball from the corner and began throwing it against the wall aggressively. Then he exploded. "I can't believe this!" he shouted, hurling the basketball at the far wall with all his force. The ball ricocheted around the room madly, sending the magazine rack flying and knocking over a tall lamp. Magazines and newspapers scattered across the floor.

"Whoa, Todd, man, take it easy," Ken said soothingly, catching the lamp and steadying it. "If you're not careful, you're going to break your other foot." He pointed to a place on the couch. "Here, have a seat." Todd sat down and stared at the wall, feeling numb.

"Listen to me for a minute, Wilkins," Ken ordered, picking up magazines off the floor and stacking them. "Elizabeth just found out about this internship, right? And she's all excited about it, right? So she makes a spur-of-the moment decision to stay at SVU. But there's no way she'll be able to do it."

"Why not?" Todd asked, picking up a bag of tortilla chips and stuffing five into his mouth at once.

"Well, the most obvious reason is that she doesn't have a high-school diploma," Ken said logically.

"GED," Todd mumbled through his chips.

"What did you say?" Ken asked. "Dee dee dee?"

Todd swallowed and took a swig of cola from a big half-empty bottle on the table. "She can take her high-school-equivalency exam."

"Uh-huh," Ken said. "Right." He stood a moment, lost in thought. "Well, what about her parents? They wouldn't let her start college already."

"She thinks they'll be thrilled for her," Todd said, his voice expressionless.

Ken sighed. "Look, Todd," he said. "There's no way she'd leave you. After all, you two have been to-gether forever. She's not just going to throw all that away for some stupid internship."

"She wants a long-distance relationship," Todd said. He slumped deeper into the couch, wishing it would swallow him up. "Weekends, holidays, summers. Phone calls." He laughed bitterly. "Some relationship."

Ken opened his mouth but then shut it, looking as if he were at a loss for words. Finally he took a seat next to his best friend. "I really feel for you, man," he said, looking over at Todd with concern. "You and Liz have been together so long, I can't imagine you two being apart."

Suddenly the color drained from Ken's face. "What about Jessica?" he asked, his voice filled with worry.

Todd shrugged. Right now Jessica Wakefield was the least of his concerns.

Late that night Todd steered his black BMW through the streets of the sleeping town, lost in thoughts of Elizabeth. He had been driving aimlessly for hours, trying to work out the frustration that was consuming him. He had flown up the coastal highway like a madman, driving at full speed with the radio blasting. Feeling calmer, he had taken a meandering route back, maneuvering the car along small back roads along the coast.

Todd flipped on the radio and fiddled with the dial until he came to a familiar tune. The lyrics "please don't go" blasted out of the speakers. Todd turned the volume down, feeling assaulted, and twisted the knob quickly. "I'm so tired of being alone," piped through the speakers. He turned the dial again, stopping at his favorite station. "A kiss is just a kiss, and . . ." Todd flipped off the radio in disgust. Didn't anyone have anything to sing about except love and relationships?

A kiss is just a kiss. A kiss is just a kiss. The tune played itself over and over again in his mind. Todd cut his speed and maneuvered the car to the right, driving past a small neighborhood park. *Our favorite tree,* Todd thought as he drove past a majestic oak. *Where we had our first kiss.* Even though it seemed like ages ago, Todd could still remember the moment vividly. The day had been bright and sunny, and Elizabeth had been like sunshine in his arms, her blond hair gleaming and her laughter joyful. And then she had lifted her face to his, and they had kissed for the first time. Todd had felt as if the world had turned upside down.

Todd smiled at the memory as he drove past the park, steering the car upward until he reached the highest elevation in town: Miller's Point, the parking spot overlooking Sweet Valley. Todd nosed the car to the edge of the lot and cut the engine, staring down at the lights twinkling like jewels in the town below. "A kiss is just a kiss," Todd sang under his breath.

He could practically feel Elizabeth in his arms. He ached to be with her again, to run his fingers through her spun-gold hair, to touch her velvety skin. How many nights had he and Elizabeth driven up to Miller's Point to be alone together? How many nights had they gazed out at the view? They had been there just last Friday night, before Elizabeth had left for SVU for a week. *For only a week?* Todd wondered. *Or forever?*

Todd threw the car into reverse and backed up abruptly, the memories almost choking him. He maneuvered his way down the road and wandered through the little winding streets of the quiet town. Suddenly he found himself on Calico Drive, driving past the Wakefield house, where he and Elizabeth had spent endless hours studying, watching videos, cooking together. The house was so familiar, it felt like home. Todd continued on, taking the habitual route to the Dairi Burger, where they had hung out with their friends after countless sporting events. The popular teenage hangout was hopping, as usual. The parking lot was jammed with cars and motorcycles, and the doorway overflowed with students waiting to be seated.

Todd watched the activity from the safety of his car, feeling like a stranger to the whole scene. All the familiar places and people seemed foreign to him now. Todd realized that Sweet Valley had no purpose for him without Elizabeth.

Why was he torturing himself like this? Todd put his foot down hard on the accelerator and peeled out of the parking lot. He had thought that driving around would make him feel more peaceful, but instead the pain was deepening inside him. As he drove home, he tried to conceive of Sweet Valley without Elizabeth in it. He imagined playing basketball without Elizabeth in the stands, walking by the *Oracle* office without her in it, and eating lunch all alone in the cafeteria. He saw himself walking by Elizabeth's locker and looking for her in vain. Everywhere he went, he would keep expecting Elizabeth to appear. And she never would.

"But, Todd, it's only two hours away," Elizabeth had said. "We'll still see each other on weekends and holidays." Todd shuddered at the thought of more weeks like this one. Each day without Elizabeth had felt like a year, and he had been counting the days until she returned, marking off the spaces in his calendar with large *X*'s. He had even made reservations at the Box Tree Cafe for Sunday night, planning to surprise her with a romantic dinner.

A sense of empty desolation washed over him, and a tear ran down his face. How could Elizabeth desert him like this? They still had two more years together at Sweet Valley High. Todd slammed his fist into the steering wheel. How could she just give it all up for a worthless position on a newspaper? Didn't he mean anything to her? *I guess not,* Todd answered himself glumly, and he began to drive home.

Chapter 3

"Jessica, I don't think I've ever seen you look so beautiful," Zach said softly, staring deep into her eyes. It was Wednesday afternoon, and Jessica and Zach were sharing a picnic on the quad. Zach's gaze was so intense that Jessica's heart caught in her throat. "Your eyes are the same color as the sky," he whispered. Then he buried his face in his hands, groaning. "I can't believe I just said that."

Jessica laughed, relieved that the tension was broken. She lifted Zach's chin to look him in the face. "And your eyes are the same color as the quad," she teased.

"I don't know if that's a compliment," Zach said, picking up a baguette and ripping off two thick hunks of bread.

"Of course it is," Jessica responded. She plucked a handful of grass and held it up. "It's a beautiful color." She examined the blades of grass carefully. "Hmm,

31

sea-green, with just a speck of gold in the center."

"OK, OK, enough," Zach said, cutting off wedges of Brie cheese and spreading them on the fresh bread. "Here, blue eyes, eat this." He handed her a thick piece of bread coated lavishly with cheese.

Jessica fought down a familiar feeling of guilt as she sank her teeth hungrily into the soft bread. Zach was so thoughtful. He had prepared an elaborate picnic of French bread, Brie cheese, red grapes, and cold pasta salad. He had even brought along a portable CD player and a handful of CDs. A familiar jazz tune piped softly from the tiny speakers.

At first being with Zach had just been fun, but now she was starting to have serious feelings for him. She knew she should tell him the truth about her age. And about Ken. She had almost summoned the courage the night before, but then she had stopped herself. He would never forgive her if he knew she had been lying to him.

When they had gone to the quaint little restaurant in the mountains on Monday night, Zach had opened up to her for the first time. Zach had told Jessica how his family had moved from upstate New York to Virginia when he'd been twelve, and he had a hard time adjusting to the new school. Zach's father worked for a big research company in Washington, and the kids had told Zach that his father was a CIA agent. They'd said that he was probably claiming to do research in Washington in order to cover up his spy work—and the worst part was that Zach's father really did have a mysterious job he couldn't discuss. Zach had started doubting his own father. "If there's one thing I hate," Zach had said at dinner, "it's dishonesty."

If there's one thing I hate, Jessica thought glumly, *it's guilt.* She forced herself to shake off her feelings of culpability. She would go back to Sweet Valley, and Zach would never know the truth. She was going to be at SVU only a week, after all. *And I should be enjoying it,* Jessica told herself. It was a beautiful, sunny day, and she was with a gorgeous, attentive guy. The college campus really was idyllic, Jessica thought, taking in the scene around her. Some guys wearing Sigma sweatshirts were playing Frisbee on the quad, a group of sorority girls were suntanning on the lawn, and a small discussion group sat in a circle nearby, talking about theories of art.

Suddenly a Frisbee whizzed over her head, and Jessica ducked to avoid it.

"Sorry about that!" one of the Sigma guys called as he ran by to retrieve the Frisbee.

A long, appreciative whistle sounded. "Hey, check out the sexy blonde!" another guy yelled.

"Hey, gorgeous, you new here?" a third guy shouted. "You want to play Frisbee?"

"No, thanks," Jessica called back. "I don't play children's games."

One of the guys came closer. "What kind of games do you play?" he asked, his voice laden with insinuation.

"Not your kind," Jessica replied.

"Ooh, the lady's got a sharp tongue!" the guy shouted. He shook his head and ran back to the game.

"Watch out for the new blonde!" one of his friends said.

Jessica laughed, enjoying the attention. She was glad she had thought to dress for the occasion. She was wearing her new salmon-colored baby-doll dress. It was casual but sexy and brought out the soft highlights in her hair. She was definitely in her element: an adoring guy by her side, admiring guys surrounding her. Zach didn't seem quite so pleased as he listened to the exchange. He was eyeing the guys playing Frisbee, a protective look on his face.

Moments later two burly Sigma guys approached them.

"Hey, did you hear about our reggae party on the quad?" one of them asked, kneeling down next to Jessica. He had tight curly brown hair and a dimple in his chin. Zach looked up at him warily, putting a possessive arm around Jessica.

"No, I didn't," Jessica said, smiling up at him.

"Well, now you have," the second guy said, handing her a small blue invitation with a Sigma insignia stamped on it. "It's Saturday night at Sigma House." He had long, straight brown hair pulled back in a ponytail and a tiny gold hoop in his left ear.

"I'm really sorry," Jessica said, treating the guy to a disappointed smile. "But I've got other plans."

"Other plans!" the guy with the ponytail said, staggering backward as if he had been hit. "But what could be more important than our reggae party?"

"The Zeta formal dinner, for one," Jessica said lightly, turning to Zach and giving him an intimate smile. Zach squeezed her hand.

The curly-haired guy groaned. "The Zeta dinner,

of course." He turned his attention to Zach. "You know, I think you guys have taken every pretty girl on campus for this dinner of yours."

Zach grinned. "We're doing our best."

"Well, you're ruining our party," the guy with the earring said. The Sigmas shook their heads ruefully and turned to walk away.

"Hey, maybe another time," the first guy called back, waving to Jessica and giving her a wink.

The second guy flashed Zach a thumbs-up.

Zach shook his head after the guys had walked away. "Jessica Wakefield, you are causing a real commotion," he said. "I think every single man on this campus has checked you out today."

Jessica beamed and then ducked her head so she wouldn't seem too conceited. "That's just because I'm new here," she said modestly.

"It's a good thing I found you when I did," Zach said, kissing her on the cheek. "Before the rest of the male population on this campus swooped down on you."

Just then a big blond guy walked by with a shaggy sheepdog by his side. He did a double take as he passed Jessica, tripping over the dog's leash and stumbling to the ground.

Zach looked up to the heavens and groaned. "See? You're a safety hazard."

Jessica giggled. "Well, you're safe with me," she reassured him. Jessica flopped on her back onto the grass and dropped a few red grapes into her mouth. She was happy to be able to spend some time with Zach without thinking about the Thetas. The sorority girls ate lunch at Theta House every day at noon, so she wouldn't have to worry about Magda for another few hours.

Just then the clock tower at the end of the quad struck one. If she were at home, she'd be in chemistry right now. College definitely beat high school, and Zach made it even better.

Jessica closed her eyes, enjoying the feel of the hot afternoon sun beating down on her face. She could just see herself at college in a few years. She'd be on the cheerleading squad and get the leading role in a few school plays. And she'd go to the most exclusive sorority events with the most popular fraternity guys. *Maybe I'll even become president of the Thetas like Mom was*, Jessica thought dreamily. *After all, leadership runs in our family*.

Zach's voice broke into her thoughts—something about blues and festivals. Jessica sat up and smiled at him. "I'm sorry, what did you say, Zach?" she asked.

"I was just saying that there's going to be an all-day blues festival at the student union on Monday," Zach repeated. "We should try to catch a few hours of it."

"That sounds great," Jessica agreed. *If I were still going to be here, that is*, she amended ruefully to herself. She sighed. Only a few more days and it was back to her old juvenile existence at Sweet Valley High. She felt she had really outgrown all that childish high-school stuff. And now she wouldn't even have Elizabeth to keep her out of trouble. Jessica couldn't imagine their home without Elizabeth in it. She sat up and reached for her plate. *It's not fair*, Jessica thought, taking an aggressive bite of pasta salad. Why did Elizabeth get to stay at SVU while Jessica still had to finish two years of high school?

Suddenly Jessica choked on her salad, hit by an idea. It was kind of crazy, but then again, most good ideas were.

"Zach, I'm really sorry," she said, jumping up and kissing him on the cheek. "I've got to go talk to Elizabeth about something really important."

She ran a few feet, then stopped and turned around. "Thanks for the picnic!" she called with a wave. Zach was looking after her, dumbfounded.

Elizabeth walked across campus, hugging her books to her chest. Her mind was spinning with all the possibilities suddenly open to her—her new internship at *The Chronicle*, broadcast journalism at the campus television station, and all the cultural activities the campus had to offer: poetry readings, foreign films, local jazz bands . . .

Professor Newkirk's praise danced in her head. She had said that Elizabeth had vastly outperformed every student in the class. She had found her essay to be insightful, thoughtful, and well written. She thought that, based on Elizabeth's talent, her internship at *The Chronicle* would turn into a regular position. *Talent*, Elizabeth repeated to herself happily. Professor Newkirk thought she had talent.

Elizabeth had proved to Felicia Newkirk that she was as good a journalist as any of the other college students—but she had wanted to prove something to herself as well. She had wanted to prove that she wasn't average.

When Elizabeth and Jessica had taken the SATs, Elizabeth had prepared as if her life had depended on it. She had studied for months in advance and had stayed up all night reviewing before the exam. Jessica, on the other hand, hadn't given the SATs a moment's thought. "It's just a stupid test," Jessica had said. She had even gone out to dinner with Ken the night before. "You're going to regret it," Elizabeth had warned her twin. But the results shocked everybody: Elizabeth's scores were far below average, and Jessica's were the second highest in the class. Elizabeth had been devastated. She had watched her entire future disappear before her eyes.

Then Jessica had been accused of cheating, and they had both retaken the test. This time Jessica had prepared like a maniac and Elizabeth had relaxed. And their scores reversed as well—Elizabeth received extremely high marks and Jessica extremely low ones. Based on her second set of scores, the school board threatened to kick Jessica out of school for cheating. But, as usual, Elizabeth came to Jessica's rescue and became her greatest defender. She knew her twin. Jessica sometimes lied, manipulated, maneuvered, and schemed—but she would never cheat. In a mock trial held in front of the entire school, Elizabeth had defended her sister and proved Jessica's innocence.

Even though Elizabeth had done well on the SATs the second time around, her confidence had been shaken. She couldn't help wondering if the first scores weren't the true reflection of her intelligence. Maybe she wasn't really very smart or creative, she had thought. Maybe she did well in school only because she applied herself. One recurring thought haunted her: Was she average? Was she doomed to mediocrity?

But winning the essay contest had helped to bolster Elizabeth's self-esteem. Now she felt like her old self again. In fact, she felt like even more than her old self—she felt as if she could conquer the world. Under Professor Newkirk's tutelage she could really go places. Maybe she would even end up as one of the journalists for the elite White House corps.

Elizabeth looked across the campus, from the pretty red-tiled academic buildings to the grassy quads, barely able to contain her excitement. She couldn't wait to start her internship that afternoon. And who knew where that would lead? She pictured herself on TV, bringing the latest-breaking stories to a mesmerized public and raising the quality of broadcast journalism. She imagined herself winning awards for her cutting-edge stories in *The Chronicle*. She envisioned herself walking across the stage of the auditorium to accept the Pulitzer prize, the youngest journalist ever to receive the honor.

Suddenly she saw a familiar well-built, dark-haired, six-foot-three frame walking across the campus, and her heart skipped a beat. *Todd!* He had come to surprise her! "Todd!" Elizabeth cried, running after him and tapping him on the shoulder. The guy turned and looked at her quizzically. It wasn't

Todd—she had never seen this guy in her life!

"Oh, sorry," Elizabeth said, blushing furiously. "I thought you were someone else."

"Hey, no problem," the guy said with a grin, sauntering away. "Happens all the time."

Of course it wasn't Todd, Elizabeth berated herself. Todd was in school. And Todd had a broken ankle. The disappointment was so strong that she felt weak. She hadn't really allowed herself to realize how much she missed her boyfriend. Todd had sounded so sad on the phone the night before, she thought guiltily. "Liz, you're leaving me?" he had asked.

"Of course I'm not leaving you, Todd," Elizabeth had explained. "I'm just moving on with my life. But we can still see each other every weekend, or almost every weekend."

"It feels like you're leaving me," Todd had repeated sadly.

Now she had to wonder. Did staying at SVU mean losing Todd? Would their relationship survive a two-year separation? Elizabeth's spirits plummeted as she pondered those difficult questions. Was the internship worth risking her relationship with Todd?

Suddenly Elizabeth's gloomy thoughts were interrupted by an excited voice calling her name. She turned in the direction of the sound. Raising her hand to her forehead to shield her eyes from the glare of the sun, she peered across the grassy quad. It was Jessica, barreling across the lawn at a hundred miles an hour.

"Liz! Liz!" Jessica yelled, running toward her and

waving madly. Elizabeth waited, unable to resist a smile. Even if Jessica could be exasperating, she always managed to cheer Elizabeth up.

"You won't believe what's happened!" Jessica exclaimed as she reached her twin. She was completely out of breath, but her eyes were sparkling.

"You've been accepted into the Thetas," Elizabeth guessed.

"No, better," Jessica replied.

Elizabeth raised an eyebrow. What could Jessica possibly think was better than getting into the Thetas? "You're officially Zach's girlfriend?" she ventured.

"No," Jessica replied again.

"I know," Elizabeth said finally. "You've won an infinite shopping allowance at Lisette's." Lisette's was the most exclusive boutique at the Sweet Valley Mall. Sometimes Elizabeth teased Jessica that she spent more time at Lisette's than she did at school.

"No, no, no!" Jessica shook her head happily

Elizabeth folded her arms across her chest and waited. "Jessica, I'm not going to be able to guess," she said with a sigh. "Just tell me."

"I'm staying, too!" Jessica burst out joyfully. Before Elizabeth could respond, Jessica chattered on. "Isn't that great, Liz? We can take the GED together, and then we can get an apartment together, a real college apartment, and we can join the Thetas together, and we can double-date sophisticated college guys. . . ." Jessica linked her arm in Elizabeth's. "I just can't live without my twin," she sang.

41

Elizabeth rolled her eyes. "You just can't live at home without someone to divert Mom and Dad's attention away from you," she said. But secretly she felt happy. College wouldn't be so lonely with Jessica around—and it would definitely be a lot more fun!

Jessica watched Elizabeth walk off across the quad, hurrying to her new internship. Her twin was wearing a tailored beige linen skirt and a crisp white blouse, a jacket thrown over her arm. She looked like a young executive. Jessica shook her head. They finally had a week of freedom to hang out on a college campus, and all Elizabeth could think about was her new position on the school newspaper. For Elizabeth college was all about journalism and cultural activities.

Sometimes Jessica couldn't believe she and Elizabeth shared the same genetic code. Ian Cooke had been falling all over Elizabeth for a week, and all Elizabeth could think of was dull-as-dirt Todd Wilkins. Not that Ian was exactly Mr. Exciting, but at least he was mature. Elizabeth was really letting a chance slip by. Didn't she realize they were surrounded by the most gorgeous, available guys in the entire state of California?

Not only was Elizabeth ignoring the entire male population at SVU, but she had shown no interest whatsoever in the Thetas, the most important sorority on campus. Jessica shook her head. Elizabeth was really burning her bridges. She kept blowing off their functions and leaving Jessica to cover for her. Magda Helperin had invited them to tea at Theta House on

Monday, and Elizabeth hadn't shown up. When the girls had questioned Jessica about it, she had come up with a fast excuse. She had told them that Elizabeth was auditioning at the new student TV station for an on-air position. They were all impressed. Then the Thetas had invited them for lunch on Tuesday, and Jessica had protected her sister again. Jessica had told Magda that Elizabeth was already on campus and couldn't be reached. Magda wasn't pleased. "If she doesn't start acting like a pledge, we'll have serious doubts about whether she's qualified to be a Theta," Magda had sniffed.

Jessica turned onto the little path that led across the campus to Steven and Billie's off-campus apartment. She wondered if it was too late for Elizabeth to salvage her reputation with the Thetas. She should really try to go to the Zeta formal dinner, Jessica thought. It was the most important social event of the year. All the Thetas would be there. If Elizabeth made a good impression on them, then maybe she would have some chance of getting into the sorority. But whom could she go with? Ian was out, because he wasn't a Zeta.

Let's see, Jessica thought, running through a list of the Zetas they had met so far. Her party had been teeming with guys from the fraternity. Jessica closed her eyes, trying to recall the scene. She had met a cute guy named Bill or Will or something. But, then, he had been a terrible dancer. And then there was a hot-looking senior who had danced on Steven's coffee table with her. His name was Daniel, and he had wild black curly hair and a nose ring. Jessica giggled at the thought of him and Elizabeth together. She racked her brain to come up with more names from the party, but she could see only faces. Jessica had also met a few of Zach's fraternity brothers at Jojo's juice bar on Sunday night. Two of them had been pretty cute—Cliff and Wright. Wright? No, Dwight. Hmm, maybe they were free. Who else? Jessica thought for a few minutes and then gave up. Those were all the Zetas she knew besides Zach.

Jessica stopped dead in her tracks. *Besides Zach,* she repeated to herself. *That's it!* she thought. Suddenly she knew the perfect date for Elizabeth— and she had figured out how she could date Zach and stay on Magda's good side. Why hadn't she thought of it before? All it was going to take was a little help from her twin. Elizabeth owed her one, anyway.

Jessica reversed her direction and turned toward the Theta House. It was time to plant some important seeds.

Chapter 4

Elizabeth walked into the office of *The Chronicle* and breathed in the atmosphere: computer keys clacking, phones jangling, the smell of newsprint in the air. Just being in the environment made her fingers itch to start working on a story. Then her mouth dropped open: a Lexis/Nexis machine sat on a desk, a stream of computer paper feeding out the top. With a Lexis/Nexis machine she could pull up stories on any topic from every major newspaper and magazine in the United States. It was a dream source of information. This was an authentic newsroom, nothing like the tiny *Oracle* office at Sweet Valley High.

You're in the real world now, Elizabeth told herself, hugging her arms around her body. She wondered what her first assignment would be. Would she get to use the Lexis/Nexis machine? Her chest tightened in anticipation as she looked around for her new boss, Cliff Petherbrook.

"Excuse me," Elizabeth said to a little man hunched over a typewriter, furiously punching the keys. "Do you know where—?" The man waved her away angrily before she could get the sentence out, muttering something about a deadline.

"Oh, sorry," Elizabeth said, hurrying away. *What was I thinking?* she berated herself. Of course she couldn't just interrupt people there. They were working under extreme deadline pressure.

Elizabeth wandered into the hall, following the aroma of freshly ground coffee into a small lounge with beverage machines and a refrigerator. There were comfortable chairs and a table in the corner, but the room was deserted. Sounds of whirring and buzzing came from the next room, which was marked COPY SHOP. Elizabeth peeked in the door. A row of copiers and a fax machine were all churning away.

Elizabeth approached a woman who was pressing buttons on the fax machine. "Excuse me," Elizabeth said. "Do you know where Mr. Petherbrook's office is?"

"Down the hall, third door on the right," she replied, without looking up.

"Thank you," Elizabeth said, a little taken aback at her rudeness.

Elizabeth found the door the woman had indicated and read the impressive-looking metal placard on it: CLIFF PETHERBROOK, EDITOR IN CHIEF. Her heart beating with excitement, she knocked crisply on the door. No answer. She knocked again. She heard something that sounded like a grunt. *I guess that's my sign to go in,* Elizabeth thought. She took a deep breath and opened the door.

Mr. Petherbrook was a middle-aged, overweight man with no neck and slicked-back silver-specked hair. He had a prominent nose and sagging jowls. A pair of striped suspenders supported his paunch, and a cigar hung out of his thin lips. He was hunched over a pile of papers and didn't look up as Elizabeth entered his office. The air was thick with blue smoke, and Elizabeth choked back a cough.

Her eyes widened as she took in the impressive decor. Mr. Petherbrook's office was stately and austere, with a massive mahogany desk, two plush black-leather armchairs, and oak bookshelves lined with important-looking files. Thick beige carpeting covered the floor, and silver-framed diplomas dotted the walls. A wide window looked out onto a panoramic view of the Sweet Valley University campus.

When Elizabeth cleared her throat, Mr. Petherbrook looked up, tapping the cigar in a big round ashtray on his desk. She smiled brightly and extended a hand. "Hello, Mr. Petherbrook," she said. "I'm Elizabeth Wakefield, the new intern."

"So you're the new intern," he said, hooking his thumbs underneath his suspenders and letting his beady gray eyes wander slowly up and down her body. He looked a little surprised as he appraised her. Elizabeth dropped her hand, and blood rushed to her face.

"You ever work on a news story before?" Mr. Petherbrook asked.

"Yes, I have," Elizabeth said indignantly, fishing around in her canvas bag for her résumé. "I write a weekly column for my high-school paper, and I've written a number of pieces for several community papers. Last summer for my internship at *The London Times,* I covered—"

Mr. Petherbrook cut her off with a wave of the hand. "It's OK, sweetheart," he said in a smarmy voice. "That was just a joke."

A joke, Elizabeth thought. *Did I miss the funny part?*

She took a deep breath and composed herself. She refused to let this slimy man frazzle her. *Maybe this is some kind of test,* she thought. A test to see if she could survive in the competitive world of journalism. Well, she would show him just how capable she was. Elizabeth sat in one of the leather chairs across from his desk and held out her résumé. "Would you like a copy of my résumé, Mr. Petherbrook?" she asked.

"Er . . . yes," he answered, taking the ivory-colored paper from her. He picked up a pair of tortoiseshell glasses from his desk and pushed them onto his nose. "So what have we got here?" he said condescendingly, peering at the résumé as if it were a colored drawing made by a child.

Elizabeth sat stiffly, her hands folded tightly in her lap, waiting for his attitude to change. She knew she had an impressive résumé. He would have to take her seriously once he saw her qualifications. She mentally ticked off her achievements: straight-A student, member of the honor society, staff writer for *The Oracle,* intern at *The London Times* . . .

"Hmm, yes, yes, Sweet Valley High, the high-school paper," he muttered, looking amused as he scanned the résumé. "Oh, so you're a sorority girl?" he asked as he reached the "Activities" section of her résumé. "Pi Beta Alpha, very nice." Elizabeth mentally kicked herself. *Why did I include that?* Pi Beta Alpha was the most exclusive sorority at Sweet Valley High, but Elizabeth was a member in name only. She had joined the group merely to please Jessica, and she had attended very few of the meetings.

"And I see you starred in a soap opera with your twin sister," Mr. Petherbrook continued. "Two of you, hmm?" He looked at her with a grotesque leer. "Maybe we could find a place here for your sister as well. Two of you sure would brighten up the atmosphere around here! He guffawed loudly and broke into a fit of coughing. "Yes, brighten up the atmosphere," he chuckled to himself, wheezing and taking a sip of water.

Elizabeth ignored him, her face burning. He was purposely picking out the few frivolous elements of her résumé to undermine her. Why had she let Jessica talk her into putting those items on it? "Liz, you sound so boring," Jessica had said. "Your résumé needs more *life*." Even her parents had agreed. They said that it was important for her to draw a well-rounded portrait of herself.

"The Young and the Beautiful," Mr. Petherbrook said, repeating the name of the soap opera Elizabeth and Jessica had starred in for a week. He looked at her again, his eyes lingering on her face. Elizabeth shivered in disgust, feeling soiled from his lecherous gaze. "Hmm, young and beautiful, yes, yes." He picked up the mug from his desk and took a swig of coffee.

Elizabeth pushed back her chair and stood up. This wasn't getting her anywhere. Clearly, she was going to have to prove herself through her work, not her résumé. "Mr. Petherbrook, I would like to know what my assignment is for today," she said in her most professional-sounding voice.

Mr. Petherbrook's gray eyes crinkled with amusement. "Your assignment, huh? Let me just think about that. In the meantime, you think you're capable of getting me a cup of coffee?" he asked. He picked up the mug and shook the filmy liquid sliding around in the bottom of it. "This one's a little old."

Elizabeth was stunned. She considered turning around and marching out of the office, telling him he could get his own coffee. How dare he? She couldn't believe people still acted so sexist in this day and age.

But Elizabeth hesitated, considering her options. If she walked out now, she would never get a permanent position on *The Chronicle*. She wouldn't be able to stay at SVU. All her hopes for an early journalism career would be destroyed. And what would Professor Newkirk say? She could hear the renowned journalist's voice in her head, dripping with disdain. "So you couldn't cut it, Ms. Wakefield? You didn't want to be just another pretty face? You think it was easy for me being the first woman in the Washington press corps?"

Just this one time, Elizabeth told herself. *Just until you get your bearings.* She picked up Mr. Petherbrook's stale cup of coffee with as much dignity as she could muster, holding her head high as she walked out of the office.

Soap opera star, sorority girl, young and beautiful, she muttered to herself angrily as she made her way to the lounge. Now she understood why Jessica felt so frustrated when nobody believed she was capable of scoring so high on the SATs. There was nothing worse than being thought of as just another pretty face.

Brighten up the atmosphere, indeed, Elizabeth fumed as she carried a steaming cup of coffee down the hall. This time she didn't knock as she walked into Mr. Petherbrook's office. She placed the coffee on his desk silently and stared at him, a defiant expression on her face.

"Thanks, sweetheart," he muttered without looking up.

"My pleasure," Elizabeth said wryly. She folded her arms across her chest and tapped her right foot, waiting for her assignment.

Mr. Petherbrook pointed to a stack of papers reaching almost to the ceiling. "Photocopy these for me, will you, honeybunch?" he instructed her. He squinted at her through his cigar smoke and gave her a jowly smile. "Do you think you can manage that? You ever use a copier before, dolly?"

Elizabeth refused to answer. She took the stack in her arms and marched out of the office.

She sighed as she laid the first sheet of paper facedown on the copier. Professor Newkirk had warned her that she'd be starting at the bottom. *Well,* she thought, pressing the start button, *this certainly is the bottom.*

"Jessica, what a nice surprise!" Darcy Grey said warmly as she opened the imposing twelve-foot wood-paneled door of the Theta House on Wednesday afternoon. "Come on in!"

Jessica stepped into the huge marble foyer of the redbrick mansion, a crystal chandelier sparkling over her head. She still had trouble believing that the girls actually lived in this majestic estate. The only people she knew who lived in mansions were her best friend, Lila Fowler, and her greatest nemesis, Bruce Patman, the richest and most arrogant guy in Sweet Valley.

Jessica wished she could show the mansion to Lila. Lila would be just as excited about joining the Thetas as she was. She could imagine them sharing a room there in two years, socializing with the girls in the parlor, eating lunch every day in the dining room, hanging out at night in the TV room.

"We were just having tea and talking about the Zeta formal," Darcy said as they walked past the curving stairway to the parlor, an elegant room decorated tastefully in warm peach tones. A fire was blazing in the hearth, and the girls were curled up comfortably on covered divans and newly upholstered armchairs, chatting together excitedly. A silver tea kettle and flowered blue china cups were laid out on the table. Two big silver platters with biscuits and buttery scones lay next to the tea.

"Hi, Jessica!" Amanda Gregory said. Amanda was a freshman English major with blond hair and warm brown eyes.

"Great outfit!" Meredith, a tall, willowy girl with

52

a mass of curly red hair, said enthusiastically.

"Thanks," Jessica replied, smiling broadly.

All the girls greeted Jessica warmly except for Magda. She was sitting on the corner of a duvet by herself, her crystal-blue eyes shooting daggers. *This doesn't look good,* Jessica thought.

"Hi, Magda," Jessica said, flashing her friendliest smile. Magda fixed her with an icy stare and looked away. *Definitely not good,* Jessica realized. Magda had obviously seen her the night before at the diner with Zach. *Well,* Jessica thought, *it's time to put my plan into action.*

"Here, Jess, have some tea," Darcy said, flipping her thick, wavy auburn hair over her shoulders and picking up the teapot. She poured Jessica a steaming cup and handed it to her.

"Thanks, Darcy," Jessica said, taking the tea and adding a few biscuits to the saucer. She walked over to Magda and plopped down next to her on the sofa. Magda looked visibly annoyed and moved over a few inches.

"How's it going?" Jessica asked brightly.

"Oh, hi, Jessica," Magda said, looking at her down her imperial nose. "What a cute little outfit you're wearing," she said, eyeing Jessica's baby-doll dress with disdain. "Did you pick that up at the mall in Sweet Valley?"

Jessica pretended not to notice the snobby undertone in her voice. "Oh, I don't know. It's just a fun little dress," she said with a wave of her hand. "So how are you?"

"Couldn't be better," Magda replied in a blasé tone. "And I suppose you are doing fabulously?"

"To tell you the truth," Jessica said, sighing dramatically, "I'm at my wit's end."

"Oh?" Magda responded, her eyes narrowing. "Are you having trouble juggling the men in your life? Is your new college man getting in the way of your little boyfriend at home?" When Jessica had come to tea at the Theta House on Monday, she had confided in Magda about her interest in a college guy. Magda had been impressed, and she had confided in Jessica as well. Magda also had her sights set on a new guy: Zach Marsden. Jessica had almost choked when she'd found out. Fortunately, she hadn't told Magda exactly which college guy she was interested in.

"Oh, that didn't work out," Jessica replied, ignoring Magda's insinuating tone. "Actually, it's my sister, Elizabeth. She's driving me crazy."

Magda yawned slightly, and Jessica continued.

"She's been flirting with every single guy at SVU," Jessica explained. "We spent the day walking around the campus, and Elizabeth felt it necessary to pick up every guy we saw. I mean, it's like she needs a constant ego boost."

"Oh, how interesting," Magda said, sounding bored. She picked up her cup of tea and took a delicate sip, holding her pinkie straight out.

"She only thinks of herself," Jessica said, prattling on. "I mean, take last night, for instance. Steven and Billie spent hours preparing a really special dinner for the four of us. Then, at the last minute, Elizabeth said she couldn't make it because she had a hot date. And she has a boyfriend back home!" Jessica shook her head in disbelief.

Magda did a double take, obviously coming to the conclusion that it was Elizabeth, not Jessica, who had been out with Zach the night before. Suddenly she was all ears. "What did you say *you* did last night?" she asked.

"Oh, I didn't go out or anything. I had dinner with Steven and Billie," Jessica said casually. "You know, just a little family get-together."

Magda's demeanor changed entirely. "Jessica, I know exactly what you mean," she said, inching over and leaning her head close to Jessica's. "I have a younger sister, and she used to compete with me for everything in high school—clothes, grades, guys. It was the worst." Magda laughed and shook her glossy black hair. "But now we're really close. You know," she said warmly, touching Jessica on the knee, "you actually remind me of her."

Jessica smiled inwardly, pleased with herself. "You're lucky to have such a good relationship with your sister," she said wistfully.

"Well, she's terrific. But I feel sorry for you— Elizabeth sounds just awful," Magda said. She smiled, her eyes bright with interest. "So tell me more about your twin. What's she like?"

"Well, let's see," Jessica began. "I would say she's basically a man chaser and a manipulator. She'll do anything to get her own way, and she doesn't care who she hurts in the process."

Magda made a clucking sound with her tongue.

"You know that party we had Saturday night?" Jessica asked. "Well, Elizabeth insisted on throwing the party behind Steven and Billie's back. There was nothing I could do. By the time we arrived at their place, Elizabeth had already invited half the guys on campus to the party." Jessica laughed in disbelief. "You know, she actually wanted to have an all-guy party! That's why I invited so many girls on Saturday."

"She would never fit in here," Magda said, shaking her head disapprovingly. "I mean, we enjoy our relationships with men here, but friendship is our number-one principle. That's the whole point of a sorority—women sticking by one another, women for women. Our motto at Theta House is 'Each man for himself, and each woman for each other.'"

"I wish Liz had a few of those scruples," Jessica said regretfully. "To tell you the truth, if Liz and I weren't identical, I wouldn't even admit she's my sister."

Magda shook her head. "You know, I had her figured all wrong," she said. "I thought she was the serious twin and you were the fun-loving one. I mean, she dresses so conservatively and everything."

"That's just an act," Jessica confided. "She almost always wears her hair up in a ponytail, you know, to give off that good-girl image." Jessica rolled her eyes. "She's got everyone fooled."

"Well, she really fooled us," Magda said, whistling under her breath. "She's the last girl I would have taken for a man chaser."

Jessica nodded her head solemnly. "You wouldn't

56

believe the number of times I've had to cover for her because she's got all tangled up in some scheme to get a guy." Jessica paused, trying to look self-sacrificing. "But you know, no matter what she does, I always remain loyal to her," she said. "I mean, she is my sister, after all."

"Well, Jessica, I think you're definitely Theta material," Magda said. "Loyalty is our cardinal rule." Jessica beamed inwardly. It looked as though her future as a Theta was made. And Elizabeth's was probably shot, she thought with a twinge of guilt. But, then, Elizabeth had no interest in being a Theta anyway. After all, she hadn't even bothered showing up for any of their functions. Jessica was probably doing her a favor. Now Elizabeth wouldn't have to go through the trouble of rushing at all.

"Hey, Magda," Amanda said, coming to the couch and sitting down next to Jessica. "None of us has had a chance to speak to Jessica."

"Yeah," Meredith teased. "You're monopolizing our new pledge."

Magda laughed brightly. "You're right," she said. "How can Jessica get to know all the girls if I take up all her time? So what are we talking about?" she asked, turning her attention to the group.

Everybody laughed. "Do you need to ask?" Amanda replied.

"Of course not," Magda said. "The Zeta dinner."

"Jessica, you should see this affair," Darcy said. "It's the social event of the year. Everybody who is anybody will be there."

"And you wouldn't believe how they do up the hall," Meredith enthused. "A gourmet meal from the best caterers in town, live jazz, champagne and caviar—" She touched her fingers to her lips and made a kissing noise.

"It sounds wonderful," Jessica said wistfully. "I wish I could go."

Magda's eyes lit up. "I've got a great idea!" she exclaimed. "I'll fix you up with one of the Zetas! Then we can double-date! It'll be perfect!"

Jessica smiled. Magda had played right into her hands. *Just perfect,* she agreed.

Enid Rollins's mouth dropped open.

Olivia Davidson's eyes bugged out.

Winston Egbert dropped his fork with a clatter.

"Elizabeth's not coming back?" they exclaimed in unison.

Todd nodded glumly and looked down, digging a fork violently into his stir-fried vegetables and chopping them up with a vengeance. Ken looked at his best friend with concern. It was Wednesday afternoon, and Ken and Todd were in the cafeteria at Sweet Valley High with the usual gang. Todd had gathered all their friends together to give them the news. He had thought he should be the one to tell them. But now, Ken realized, Todd didn't feel like talking about it at all.

It was time for Ken to take over. "Elizabeth got a really good internship at the campus newspaper," he explained, "so she decided to take the GED and start college early." Suddenly everyone starting talking at once.

"She's leaving *The Oracle*?" Olivia Davidson, a stylish girl with hazel eyes and frizzy brown hair, asked. Olivia was the arts editor of *The Oracle*.

"She's abandoning all her friends?" Elizabeth's best friend, Enid Rollins, asked sadly.

"She's staying at college for a *job*?" Maria Santelli chimed in, her eyes wide with shock. Maria was one of Elizabeth's closest friends and a member of the cheerleading squad.

"I don't know," Winston said doubtfully. He put his arm around his girlfriend, Maria. "Do you really think she'd stay at SVU just for a newspaper internship? Is she getting paid?"

"That doesn't matter," Olivia said, pulling out a container of chicken salad from her lunch bag. "Liz would stay just for the experience. You know how driven she is. She wants to be a journalist more than anything in the world." She lifted a forkful of salad to her mouth.

"She thinks this internship can lead to a full-time position," Ken explained. "And it looks like she might be able to work with a really well-known journalist—Felicia Newkirk or somebody."

"Felicia Newkirk?" Olivia breathed. "I don't blame her for staying."

"Who's that?" Winston asked, dumbfounded. He picked up his grilled-cheese sandwich and took a large bite.

Olivia looked at him in shock. "You've never heard of Felicia Newkirk?"

"Hey, guys, back me up," Winston said, looking around the table for support. "Have any of you heard of Felicia Newport?" They all shook their heads.

"New*kirk*," Olivia corrected Winston. "She did a groundbreaking piece on John F. Kennedy after his assassination."

"Whew!" Winston said in appreciation. "Pretty impressive!" He clapped Todd on the back. "It looks like your girlfriend's going places."

"Looks like it," Todd mumbled.

"Well, that sounds pretty fishy to me," red-haired Caroline Pearce interrupted. All eyes turned to her. Caroline had an infamous reputation as the class gossip. If there was any good dirt floating around the school, it was pretty likely that Caroline knew all the details. "I think there's probably another reason why Elizabeth's staying."

Todd turned a hot face toward Caroline. "What are you suggesting, Pearce?" he asked angrily.

"I'm not suggesting anything, *Wilkins*," Caroline replied sweetly. "I was just wondering if perhaps she met another guy. A college guy."

Ken wheeled on Caroline, his eyes blazing. It was bad enough that Todd was miserably lonely without Elizabeth—he didn't need to be suspicious as well. "That's ridiculous," Ken snapped. "You have no idea what you're talking about. If you're going to spread such a stupid rumor, you better have a good source."

"Yeah, Caroline," Enid agreed, her voice full of annoyance. "You better watch out before you start slandering Elizabeth's character—all her best friends at this school are sitting right here in front of you, and we're not going to stand for it."

"Hey," Caroline whined. "You don't all have to jump on me. It was just a suggestion."

"Well, it was a bad one," Todd said angrily, pushing his chair back and standing up. "See you guys later." He swung his backpack over his shoulder and strode away, limping on his cast.

Ken's eyes clouded over with worry as he watched Todd storm off. His best friend was taking this really hard, he thought. But, then, who could blame him? Ken would fall apart as well if he received the kind of phone call Todd had. He would be devastated if Jessica told him she wasn't coming back to Sweet Valley.

Ken tried to picture Sweet Valley without Jessica in it, but he couldn't begin to form an image. Sweet Valley and Jessica Wakefield just seemed to go together. In fact, he could barely remember what Sweet Valley had been like before he and Jessica had started dating, even though they'd been together for only a short time.

Jessica and Ken had been friends for as long as he could remember. They had got even closer while Jessica was dating Jeremy Randall, an environmentalist from New York. Everybody had been a little surprised that Jessica was dating an older guy, but they had been totally stunned when she had got engaged to him. It turned out that the whole engagement was a scam. Jeremy had just been using Jessica to get to his former fiancée's inheritance. Jessica had gone through a really difficult time, and Ken had helped her through it. Then suddenly, out of nowhere, a spark had ignited between them—a spark that soon flamed into a hot romance.

Ken gazed into space, images of their relationship flashing through his mind like scenes in a movie: lying on a deserted strand of beach sharing a romantic picnic by moonlight; cuddling together on the couch in Ken's living room watching Jessica's favorite movie, *Gone with the Wind;* savoring the triumph of Ken's winning touchdown at the Big Mesa game as Jessica cheered him on from the sidelines; running through the pouring rain together to Ken's car after the game, holding hands and laughing. . . .

Everybody said they were the perfect couple, the cocaptain of the cheerleading squad and the star quarterback of the football team, both blond and popular. Ken felt that he was part of a team now, and that one half—Jessica—was missing. This week had been lonely enough for him to know that Sweet Valley High with no Jessica Wakefield wouldn't really be Sweet Valley High at all.

Chapter 5

Jessica leaned back against the sofa bed in Steven and Billie's apartment Wednesday evening, blowing on her freshly painted nails. The brown velveteen couch looked like a beauty salon, littered with cosmetics, women's magazines, and an assortment of hair products. Jessica hugged her knees to her chest, thinking dreamily about her date with Zach that evening. He wanted to drive up the coast and take a moonlight walk on the beach.

Unfortunately, a nagging thought in the back of her mind kept interrupting her reverie. Ken. She had to tell him about her decision to stay, and she wasn't looking forward to it. She looked over at the red rose Ken had given her, wilting in a vase on the nightstand. Ken and Todd had surprised the twins before they'd left, showing up at the Wakefield house unexpectedly with fluffy blue SVU sweatshirts. And Ken had given Jessica a single red rose. A wave of guilt washed over her as she looked at the drooping flower. And now she was two-timing Ken.

Jessica sighed, trying to shake her guilty feelings. She hadn't meant for anything to happen with Zach. She had thought it was only an innocent flirtation. But then the relationship had just sort of developed on its own. It *was* exciting to be with an older man, especially one who appreciated her intelligence as well as her looks.

When she had told Ken how high she'd scored on the SATs, he hadn't believed her. "Right, Jessica," he had said sarcastically. Then, when she had been accused of cheating, Elizabeth had been the only one who had stood by her. Heather Mallone had kicked her off the cheerleading squad, and Amy Sutton and Maria Santelli had gone along with Heather. Even Ken hadn't believed she was smart enough to have pulled off such high test scores on her own. "C'mon, Jessica, you can tell me the truth," he had said to her one night at Miller's Point. Jessica had been furious.

Eventually Ken had come around. When Elizabeth had held a mock trial in the assembly hall to prove Jessica's innocence, Ken had stood behind her. He'd even rallied the whole football team to show their support for her. But, still, Jessica couldn't quite lose the feeling that Ken didn't think she was very smart.

Then she had met Zach. Zach appreciated all of her—her looks and her mind. He hadn't even blinked when she'd told him she was a transfer from Princeton. "Pretty and intelligent," Zach had said appreciatively. For the first time in her life Jessica felt like a whole person with someone she was dating. Because Zach was mature and in college, Jessica told herself, he was secure enough to accept the possibility that a woman could be as smart as he was.

Jessica looked at the phone sitting on the coffee table. *Call Ken!* it seemed to be saying. "Not yet—later," she told the phone. She picked up a fashion magazine and flipped through the pages. *You have to call him now!* the phone seemed to scream, drawing her attention away from the magazine. Jessica groaned, threw the phone to the floor, and shoved it under the couch.

I'll call him tomorrow, she promised herself. That way she would get a good night's sleep and would have more time to decide what to say. But she knew she should get it over with. After all, Jessica had already told Lila that she was staying, and it would be better if Ken heard the news from Jessica. Jessica sighed as she thought of her conversation with Lila. Her best friend hadn't been pleased. In fact, it had barely been a conversation. Lila had hung up on her.

"OK, OK, I'll call him," Jessica mumbled to herself, scrambling to the floor and reaching for the phone under the couch. She plopped down in a fraying blue armchair and punched in Ken's number, hoping he wouldn't be home.

"Hello?" Ken answered eagerly on the first ring.

"Ken?" Jessica asked tentatively.

"Jess!" Ken breathed, his voice warm. "I've been thinking about you all day! How's my college woman doing?"

Jessica winced at Ken's use of the possessive. He

sounded so sweet and caring. "I'm doing great," Jessica said, forcing a light tone to her voice. "I've been meeting a lot of the Theta girls—and they seem to have accepted me."

"I bet you're already in—two years ahead of schedule," Ken said.

Jessica laughed. "I am making a pretty good impression. One of the girls said I was definitely Theta material." She picked up the phone and walked over to the couch, fishing through the array of cosmetics. Cradling the phone in the crook of her right shoulder, she grabbed a stick of lipstick and began carefully lining her lips.

"That's my girl!" Ken said enthusiastically. "One week on the college campus and she's already a member of the best sorority at SVU." Jessica felt a pain in her heart. She had forgotten how supportive Ken could be.

"So what's going on at school?" she asked, pulling a tissue out of the dispenser on the side table and blotting her lips.

"Well, all anybody is talking about is your sister," Ken said. "What's this about Elizabeth not coming back? Todd is walking around like his life is over."

Jessica took a deep breath and paced the room, the phone line trailing behind her. "It's true," she told Ken. "Elizabeth decided that she shouldn't wait to launch her journalism career. She got this great opportunity on the college newspaper, and she might be able to work with a really famous journalist."

"Well, I guess she's got to do what's best for her," Ken said. He paused for a moment. "But now for the most important question—when are *you* coming back?"

"Uh, well . . ." Jessica stammered, twisting the phone cord around her hand nervously. "That's why I'm calling, actually."

"You're not coming back, either," Ken said in a flat voice, as if he had expected it all along.

"Right," Jessica said in a shaky voice, falling into the chair again. Ken was silent, and static filled the line. Suddenly Jessica felt panicky. She grabbed the receiver, holding it close to her ear. What was Ken doing? Was he crying?

"Ken, are you there?" Jessica asked.

"Yeah, I'm here," Ken replied in a low voice.

"It's just that—oh, Ken—there are so many opportunities for me here," Jessica said, the words coming out in a rush. "I can join the Thetas, the cheerleading squad, the school plays—"

Ken cut her off. "But you can do all that in two years when you start college. Don't you think you're getting a little ahead of yourself?"

"It's more than that," Jessica explained. "I can't leave Elizabeth here all alone. I mean, she is my twin sister. And it looks like we can get an off-campus apartment together. There's even one available in Steven's building."

There was a long silence on the other end of the line. When Ken spoke, his voice sounded raw. "Oh, Jess," he whispered, "I don't want to hold you back from your life, but I don't know how I'll make it here without you." His voice cracked. "Sweet Valley just isn't the same when you're not here."

Jessica's heart dropped at the sadness in his voice. Suddenly she remembered all the reasons why she loved him. Ken was caring, tender, thoughtful, and incredibly handsome. A sharp pang of guilt stabbed her in the chest.

The doorbell rang. "Ken, I've gotta go, OK?" Jessica said.

"Wait, Jess!" Ken exclaimed. "Can't we talk about this?"

"Tomorrow, OK?" Jessica said, and she hung up the phone.

Jessica took a deep breath, feeling a little shaky about her decision as she made her way down the hall. She plastered a smile on her face as she opened the door. Then she looked into Zach's intense green eyes, and the smile deepened into a genuine grin.

> "The wall is gone
> without a trace
> a trail of dust
> and dusty memories.
> In my mind's eye
> the wall is there
> a stony border
> behind my eyelids.
> How can I see beyond it?
> How can I get my thoughts around it?
> I cannot grasp it.
> I am the fossil
> of history's lessons.
> I am the remnant

68

of history's games.
It is sublime.
I cannot grasp it.
The wall is gone
but the wall in my mind
is an ever-present
structure.
How can I
chip it
away?"

Elizabeth held her breath, engrossed in the power of the words, as the German student finished reciting his poem. She was sitting with Ian and a group of students at the campus coffee bar, a dark and cramped café with redbrick walls and candlelit wooden tables. She applauded enthusiastically with the rest of the crowd. It was Wednesday night—poetry-reading night at the coffee bar.

"Thank you," the student said, bowing his head modestly and stepping down from the microphone. Ian had given Elizabeth a quick biography of the poet before he'd begun. His name was Friedrich Keller, and he'd emigrated to the United States in 1990 after the Berlin Wall had come down. He was putting together a collection of poems entitled *The Wall* about growing up in East Berlin during the Stalinist regime.

"Wow, he's really good," Elizabeth said to Ian, feeling somewhat awed.

Ian nodded. "He's quite talented," he said. "His poetry has a particularly raw quality."

"That's exactly it!" Elizabeth said, excited. "It's honest and direct. He's not afraid to reveal himself."

"I thought you would enjoy it," Ian said. He touched her hand in a friendly gesture and smiled. "I'm glad you could make it here tonight." Elizabeth smiled back, relieved to see that Ian appeared to be accepting their friendship. When they had first met, he'd been interested in dating her. Elizabeth had told him right away that she had a serious boyfriend, but he hadn't seemed to have got the message. A few days before, when he had tried to take her hand, Elizabeth had abruptly pulled out of his grasp. After that Ian had been somewhat cold and distant. But now it looked as if he was back to normal.

The poem reverberated in Elizabeth's mind. A few of the lines returned to her: "The wall is gone/but the wall in my mind/is an ever-present/structure." As if the memory of Friedrich's past was stronger than the reality of his present. *What was it like growing up in East Berlin?* Elizabeth wondered. What was it like growing up in an oppressive regime that you couldn't escape? *"How can I chip it away?"* How did one heal from a past like that?

Elizabeth's mind was buzzing with ideas as she took in the atmosphere around her. The coffee bar seemed to draw a really interesting crowd. Most of the students looked like left-wing, radical types, wearing cutoff jeans, tie-dyed T-shirts, and Birkenstocks. A group of punky-looking kids were sitting at a round table in the corner. They had dyed red and green hair and nose rings. Elizabeth felt energized as she thought of the intellectual possibilities suddenly open to her. *Will I ever have the courage to recite one of my poems here?* she wondered.

"That was depressing," Anne, a striking Asian-American woman with short, poker-straight black hair, told Elizabeth and Ian. "Particularly in light of what's still going on in China today."

"Last week's poem was much more positive," Willis said. He was a cute guy with long golden hair pulled back in a ponytail. "About freedom in the face of adversity and the value of Marxist thought."

Just then the waiter showed up with their order, setting down espressos and cappuccinos on the table. He placed thick slices of carrot cake in front of Willis and Ian, and a bowl of mixed nuts in the middle of the table. Striking a match, he lit a low white candle and set it down, bathing the table in a warm golden light.

"I think communism is the only humanitarian system there is," Maria, a woman with small, round wire-framed glasses and thick, curly hair wrapped up in a bandanna, said to the group. She dropped a brown-sugar cube into her coffee and stirred.

"Look what happened in Russia," Ian scoffed, slicing into his carrot cake.

"That was totalitarianism, not Marxism," Maria insisted, taking a sip of her espresso.

"I think Maria's right," Jay interjected. Jay was an African-American guy with a small silver hoop in his left ear. "According to Marx, in a truly communist system, one will be free to fish in the morning, hunt in the afternoon, and philosophize in the evening."

"And in a truly capitalist system, you're free to get up every day and go to a nine-to-five job," Ian said, picking up his cappuccino. Everybody laughed.

Elizabeth was getting more and more excited as the conversation swirled about her. This was the kind of discussion she had always dreamed she would have at college. She could just imagine trying to talk like this at the cafeteria at Sweet Valley High. Everybody would laugh at her.

"I think the value of capitalism is freedom," Elizabeth put in, stirring her cappuccino thoughtfully.

They all looked at her as if she were an idiot.

"Freedom?" Maria scoffed. "Freedom to do what? To run around in circles buying and selling the latest goods produced by the market?"

"Haven't you read Marx's critique of capital in *The Grundrisse*?" Willis asked.

"Or the Frankfurt School's critique of mass consumer culture?" Jay added, reaching for a handful of nuts.

"Everybody knows that our so-called freedom is just a way to keep us enslaved to the capitalist machine," Anne said.

"Yeah, we spend all our time buying things, fixing them, and protecting them," Willis agreed. He took a big bite of carrot cake and offered it around.

"It's such an insidious mechanism," Maria said, taking a forkful of cake from Willis's plate. "We're all indoctrinated by the media and advertisements."

"And the media is controlled by the white male power elite," Anne added. She scooped up a handful of nuts and dropped a few into her mouth.

"Of course," Jay agreed. "Freedom in the United States is just a way to keep the power structure intact."

Elizabeth recoiled from the assault, wishing the wooden floor of the café would open and swallow her up. She had never been so humiliated in her life—or so at a loss for words. They were all looking at her in disgust, waiting for her response. But Elizabeth didn't even know what they were talking about. *The Grundrisse?* The Frankfurt School? She glanced over at Ian, sending a silent message for help.

"I think Elizabeth's talking from a journalistic perspective," Ian said smoothly. Elizabeth swallowed hard and nodded silently. "She's referring primarily to First Amendment rights, to freedom of speech and integrity of reporting."

"Do you think First Amendment rights promote freedom in every case?" Willis wondered.

"Yeah, what about hate speech?" Jay asked pointedly. "Doesn't that just perpetuate racial hatred?"

"Or sexual harassment," Anne added. "When I hear 'free' sexist remarks on the street, it doesn't feel like freedom to me."

Elizabeth breathed a sigh of relief as their attention turned away from her. She could still feel her face burning in the darkened room. She had thought she had received a well-rounded education, but she clearly had a lot to learn. If she wanted to enroll at SVU now, she was going to have to take a crash course in literature and philosophy. Elizabeth made a firm resolve. By the time she started classes at SVU, she was going to be at a college level. She was going to spend every

73

spare moment reading theory and philosophy.

After she had been attacked for her opinion, the night seemed interminable. Elizabeth sat in tense silence, afraid to contribute a word. Finally the meeting broke up. As she and Ian walked across campus, Elizabeth gave voice to her humiliation. "I've never been so embarrassed in my whole life," she said.

"Don't worry about it," Ian reassured her, draping a friendly arm around her shoulder. "You just hit on a touchy issue."

"I guess so," Elizabeth said, unconvinced. "But I'm really beginning to doubt myself. My internship today was so disappointing."

"How so?" Ian asked.

"I guess you could say it was my first introduction to slave labor," Elizabeth said, making a wry face. "I spent the whole time at the photocopy machine. And getting coffee for my boss."

Ian laughed. "Well, what did you expect?" he asked. "To win some more awards and become an overnight sensation?"

Elizabeth bit her lip. That sort of *was* what she had expected.

"Elizabeth, in the real world you've got to fight your way to the top," Ian said patiently. "You can't just expect to get respect for nothing. You've got to earn it."

Ian's right, Elizabeth thought. *I'm so naive.*

"This is the worst," Todd said, tossing a football to Ken.

"The worst," Ken agreed, catching the ball and returning it halfheartedly.

It was Wednesday evening, and Ken and Todd were moping around Ken's house. Ever since Jessica had broken the news to him that she was staying at SVU, Ken had been pacing around his living room, unable to concentrate on anything. He couldn't sleep, he couldn't study—even working out didn't help him get his mind off Jessica. Finally he had called Todd. If misery loves company, he had thought, then Todd was definitely the right person to invite over.

"Hey, didn't you have football practice today?" Todd asked suddenly.

"I blew it off," Ken said, his voice filled with disgust. "I mean, what's the use? Football doesn't have much meaning without Jessica around. I can just imagine throwing a winning pass and looking at the sidelines to see that ice princess, Heather Mallone, leading the cheer." He shuddered.

"I know what you mean," Todd said. "It's just as well that I'm out for the season. I can't imagine playing without Elizabeth in the stands to cheer me on." Todd balanced the football on his index finger and twirled it around.

"And we wouldn't be able to go out with the twins after the games to celebrate anyway," Ken said, his glum face getting even glummer.

"No more burgers and shakes at the Dairi Burger," Todd said, lobbing the ball to Ken.

"No more ice-cream sundaes at Casey's," Ken added, catching the football under his arm and lobbing it back.

"No more nights at Miller's Point," Todd said.

"No more nights at Miller's Point," Ken echoed. The thought was so horrifying that they both collapsed onto the couch and lapsed into silence.

Suddenly the doorbell rang. "Maybe it's Jessica," Ken said, jumping up and flying down the hall. *Maybe she changed her mind and sped back home to tell me,* he thought hopefully.

Ken flung the front door open in anticipation. Then his heart dropped to his feet. It was Lila, with Enid standing behind her.

"Oh, hi," Ken said, barely managing a wave. "C'mon in." He walked into the living room. Todd was still sitting despondently on the couch, flipping the football in the air.

Lila strode into the living room and whipped off her sunglasses. She glanced from Todd's miserable face to Ken's. "You two are pathetic," she said. "Is this the best you can do—sit around and feel sorry for yourselves?"

"Do you have a better suggestion, Lila?" Ken asked, annoyed. The last thing he needed was Lila Fowler's obnoxious comments.

"Yes, I do," Lila replied, flipping her hair over her shoulder. "We need a plan."

"Lila, it's ten o'clock at night," Todd said, reading the big wooden clock on the wall of the Dairi Burger. "Don't you think it's a little late for sunglasses?" Todd, Ken, Lila, and Enid had decided to convene at the popular hangout to come up with a "Get the Wakefield Twins Back to Sweet Valley High" plan.

76

Todd was glad that Lila had the initiative to come up with a scheme, but he wasn't thrilled at the idea of working with her. Snobby Lila had never been his favorite person.

Lila slowly removed her black cat-shaped, diamond-studded sunglasses. Twirling the stem with one finger, she looked down her nose at Todd. "Todd, you don't know the first thing about fashion," she said in her most imperial tone.

Todd snorted. "Yeah, but I do know something about *light*," he snickered.

Lila's thin eyebrows came together in a perfect arch. "Do you boys want our help or not?"

"Of course we do," Ken said, kicking Todd under the table. "Sorry, Lila. Todd's just feeling a little under the weather. You understand."

"Hmmph," Lila murmured with a flick of her hair.

Just then the waiter arrived. None of them had much of an appetite, so they all ordered fries and shakes.

As soon as the waiter was out of earshot, Lila beckoned for the group to lean in toward her. "I was thinking on the way over, and I think I've got an idea," she whispered. "Todd, remember when I thought the Wakefields were being held hostage?"

Todd moaned. "How could I forget?" Lila had misunderstood Jessica on the phone when Sue Gibbons, Jeremy Randall's ex-fiancée, had been kidnapped. Lila had thought the entire Wakefield family was being held hostage, and Lila and Todd had come up with an elaborate plan to rescue the family. The results had been disastrous. There was no way he was going to let Lila talk him into another crazy idea like that.

"Well?" Lila pressed.

Todd practically exploded. "You want to kidnap the twins?"

"Sure, why not?" Lila asked with a slight smile. "It'll be a friendly kidnapping. Just till we get them back where they belong."

"And then we can deprogram them, like they do to people who have been kidnapped by a cult," Enid added. "We'll make Jessica and Elizabeth realize that they truly belong here, with us."

"Nope, it'd never work," Ken said.

"Why not?" Enid asked.

"Jessica," Ken and Todd said together.

"The minute anybody tries to force Jessica into anything, she becomes even more determined to get her own way," Ken explained. "She'd be back at SVU so fast, we wouldn't even know we'd seen her."

Lila sighed. "You're so right. Kidnapping won't work. We're going to have to come up with another— oh!" she exclaimed as the waiter suddenly appeared, placing a strawberry shake and a plateful of fries in front of her. He gave her an odd look and set down the rest of the food hastily, looking nervous. They all burst into laughter as he walked away.

"Maybe he's worried we're going to kidnap him," Lila said, picking up a fry and drenching it in ketchup.

"And hold him hostage for all his tip money," Enid added, taking a long sip of her root-beer float.

"Hmm," Ken murmured, deep in thought.

"Maybe we can't kidnap them, but we could sabotage their college experience."

"That's an idea," Todd said. If they could make Jessica and Elizabeth decide they hated college, then they'd turn around and come back on their own.

"Let's see," Ken began. "First of all, we'd have to ruin Elizabeth's internship." He stuffed a handful of fries into his mouth.

"And we'd have to sabotage Jessica's chances of becoming a Theta," Todd put in.

But Enid was shaking her head. "No, that's too extreme," she said. "We might succeed in getting them back here, but they'd never speak to us again."

"And we don't want to destroy their entire future," Lila said, taking a delicate sip of her strawberry shake. "I'm planning to room with Jessica at Theta House in a few years."

"Well, then, why don't we use the oldest ploy in the book?" Ken suggested.

All eyes turned to him expectantly. "Guilt," he said.

Todd pondered that for a moment. "Guilt might work," he said. "In fact, I think Elizabeth's already feeling really bad about the whole thing."

"If we laid it on thick it enough, she'd be sure to come back," Enid put in.

"No, that won't work," Lila said with a dismissive wave of her perfectly manicured hand. "Guilt only works for one Wakefield twin."

Ken nodded. "Lila's right. Jessica has an uncanny way of justifying everything in her head."

Finally Todd gave up. "Aww, forget it," he said. "If they don't care about us anymore, they can just stay there."

Suddenly Lila's eyes lit up. "That's it!" she breathed.

Todd looked at her as if she were crazy. "Lila, I didn't really mean that."

"Exactly!" Lila exclaimed.

Todd was more confused than ever. But it looked as if Ken and Enid were beginning to catch on.

"Not a bad idea," Ken said, nodding.

"Reverse psychology," Enid said. "Brilliant."

They hunched together and talked excitedly about how they would put their plan into action.

"And everybody has to be in on it," Lila added as their meeting broke up. "Mr. and Mrs. Wakefield, Steven and Billie, and the whole cheerleading squad."

"Of course," Enid said. "We can't let them think they have even one ally left at Sweet Valley High."

Chapter 6

"The ocean looks angry tonight," Zach said, taking Jessica's hand as they strolled along the water's edge on Wednesday evening. Jessica and Zach stopped and gazed out at the sea together. The ocean was a deep blue-green with high rollers and frothing whitecaps. A violent tumult of waves billowed and rolled, swelling up, then crashing down in explosions of white foam.

"It's like a furious old man raging at the world," Jessica mused, slipping off her shoes and holding them in her free hand. She could feel tiny waves breaking under her feet.

"That's just what my mother used to say," Zach said. "That the sea was like a person, reflecting the mood of the world." He looked pensive as he spoke. "It could be a wise old woman, or an angry man, or a mischievous little boy—"

"Or a handsome young man," Jessica interrupted,

standing up on her tiptoes and kissing Zach on the cheek. Zach smiled and gave her hand a squeeze.

Zach became pensive as they continued walking. "I think my best memories are of the time I spent at the ocean," he reminisced. "We used to go to the Jersey shore every summer when I was little. To Ocean City. There was nothing better than walking on the damp boardwalk smelling the salty sea air."

"I love boardwalks," Jessica said. "Especially when they've got amusement parks underneath them." Then she regretted her words. Did that sound too juvenile?

"Me, too," Zach said, wrapping an arm around her. "I used to love riding the Ferris wheel at Ocean City. It seemed like you could see the end of the world over the ocean. Do you know the one I'm talking about?"

Jessica gulped and shook her head. This was dangerous territory. Whenever Zach started talking about life on the East Coast, Jessica got nervous, since she had told him she'd spent part of her life there.

"But you've been to Ocean City, right?" Zach pressed.

"Actually, no, I've never been there," Jessica admitted.

Zach was astounded. "You went to Princeton and you never went to the shore? But you must at least have gone to Atlantic City."

"Oh, well, Atlantic City, of course," Jessica said, bluffing. At least she had heard of it. "One weekend a bunch of us drove down for the weekend and went gambling."

"How'd you do?" Zach asked.

"Let's just say I had to borrow money for lunch the next day," Jessica told him with a grin.

Zach laughed. "Look," Jessica said, pointing out to sea, "somebody's surfing out there." She looked over at Zach with a smile, trying to change the subject to a safer topic. "Weren't you telling me about your surfing exploits the other day?"

Zach let out a low whistle as he watched the surfer ride a cresting wave. "I wouldn't last a minute in waves like this," he said, shaking his head in admiration. "That guy's really good." Zach paused, thinking back. "The most dangerous surfing experience I had was at Ocean City. . . ."

Jessica tuned Zach out, relieved that she had got through another tight spot. It was nerve-racking having to watch every word she said. If she made the slightest slip, then the whole truth could come out. And after all his talk about honesty, Zach would never forgive her for lying to him.

But, then, Jessica reassured herself, she didn't have to worry about it. It looked as if she had the situation under control. At this point she had had enough close calls with Zach to realize that she could handle almost any situation that arose. She had definitely succeeded in convincing Zach that she was a college student. And it seemed as if she had the Magda problem handled as well—as long as she could convince Elizabeth to help her out.

"You're so special, Jessica," Zach said suddenly, stopping and turning toward her, his handsome face outlined in the moonlight. Jessica's heart skipped a beat.

"Most girls at SVU are so caught up in classes and their sororities that they won't spend any quality time with a guy," Zach said, brushing back a golden strand of hair from her face. "I'm glad you're not like that."

Zach pulled her toward him and kissed her passionately. Breathless, Jessica gazed into his eyes. But suddenly she saw Ken in front of her. Ever since she'd heard Ken's voice on the phone, she hadn't been able to get him out of her mind. Jessica shook her head, trying to clear the image. Why was she thinking about a high-school boy at home when she had a college man right there who was crazy about her?

"Liz?" an excited female voice said over the phone.

"Enid!" Elizabeth exclaimed, flopping down onto the couch and placing the phone on her stomach. It felt so good to hear her best friend's voice. She hadn't realized how much she missed sharing her life with her best friend. "I've got so much to tell you!"

"I know!" Enid squealed. "I heard! You're not coming back!"

Elizabeth stared at the receiver, perplexed. Why did Enid sound so happy? She had thought she would be excited for her—but not this excited.

Enid prattled on. "Oh, Liz, I think this internship will be so great for you! We're all really thrilled for you here. Just think, you're really going to start your adult life! No more silly high-school parties, no more bad hamburgers and shakes at the Dairi Burger, no more fattening ice-cream sundaes at Casey's, no more juvenile football games, no more petty little high-school newspaper stories. . . ."

Elizabeth's heart sank as Enid chattered on. No more high-school parties, no more football games, no more nights at the Dairi Burger, no more stories for *The Oracle*. . . . Each item Enid rattled off felt like a blow.

"You're really in the big leagues now, Liz!" Enid said cheerfully.

"Enid, do you really think I made the right decision?" Elizabeth asked, suddenly thrown into confusion. She sat up and leaned back against the couch, twirling the phone cord distractedly.

"Well, *I* would be a little scared," Enid confessed. "But I'm sure you know what you're doing." Elizabeth pondered that for a moment. Had she been too hasty in her decision? Was she in over her head?

"Liz, I've been dying to tell you what's been going on at school," Enid chatted excitedly. "You know that community edition of *The Oracle* that you and Olivia worked so hard on?"

"How could I forget?" Elizabeth said with a laugh. The paper had run a special edition covering homeless people and housing projects in the greater California area. Working as a photojournalism team, Elizabeth and Olivia had spent weeks combing the area for interesting material.

"Well, Olivia's paste-up for the piece won first prize at the community center, and they're doing an exhibit of the photographs there next week."

"You're kidding!" Elizabeth exclaimed. "That's fabulous!"

"But that's not the half of it," Enid continued. "Harry was so jealous, he said the photographs only won because of the worthy subject matter. Olivia was furious. She told him he wasn't worthy subject matter and broke up with him."

Elizabeth gasped. "Olivia and Harry broke up?" she asked. Olivia and Harry Minton had been an item ever since he had posed as an art collector to get to know her, buying one of her paintings for a thousand dollars. Harry was a student at an art school in the area and always seemed a little envious of Olivia's natural talent.

"Actually," Enid confided, "I don't think the breakup will last. I think it'll all blow over after the exhibit, and then Harry will come crawling back on his hands and knees offering to buy all the photographs."

Elizabeth burst out laughing. "I wouldn't be surprised," she said.

"And then—oh, but what am I thinking?" Enid said, stopping herself. "You're not interested in all this childish gossip."

Suddenly Elizabeth felt starved for all the Sweet Valley High news. Enid sounded so young and carefree—and Elizabeth felt so burdened with responsibility.

"Of course I'm inter—" Elizabeth started to protest, but Enid chattered on.

"You know, I really think it's all for the best," Enid

interrupted. "I mean, we'll get to see each other on vacations, and we can always talk on the phone."

"But, Enid . . ." Elizabeth ventured, suddenly feeling neglected. "Aren't you going to miss me?"

"Of course I'm going to miss you!" Enid said. "But I'm trying to look on the bright side of things. Maybe this is a good thing for me as well."

"How so?" Elizabeth asked cautiously.

"Now *I'll* be the smartest girl at Sweet Valley High!" Enid exclaimed. Elizabeth stared at the receiver in consternation.

"Oh, and Liz, one more thing," Enid said.

"Yes?" Elizabeth asked.

"Would you mind if I took over your 'Personal Profiles' column at *The Oracle*?"

Elizabeth flipped onto her side and wrapped the sheet around her body, careful not to wake Jessica, who was lying beside her on the sofa bed. Elizabeth had been tossing and turning for the past half hour, trying to find a comfortable position. But she was too wound up to fall asleep. The conversation she'd had earlier with Enid was haunting her. She was leaving her entire high-school life behind—Enid, Todd, her parents, *The Oracle*. . . . Elizabeth bit her lip, asking herself the same question that had been on her mind all evening: Was she making the right decision?

But then she thought of *The Chronicle* and the campus broadcast TV station. She was sure her internship would get better if she just stuck it out. And maybe she could work under the guidance of

Felicia Newkirk. Elizabeth rolled around to her other side and hugged the pillow to her body, her stomach tightening in excitement as she thought about the possibilities open to her.

"Liz," Jessica whispered. "Are you up?"

"Am I up?" Elizabeth said, flicking on the lamp. "I haven't been able to sleep at all."

"Me either," Jessica told her twin. "I'm too excited to fall asleep."

Jessica sat up, her blond hair tousled around her face. She was wearing Ken's football shirt, a red jersey with number 78 on the front. "Liz, I am totally psyched," Jessica said enthusiastically. "I can't believe we're actually going to be real college students with our own apartment. We can have friends over all the time, and we can throw huge parties."

Elizabeth groaned and buried her head under the pillow. "Jessica, how am I going to get any work done?"

"Is that all you can think about?" Jessica demanded. "Don't worry, you'll have your own room. You can sit in front of your computer all night while I entertain our guests."

"But you'll trash the rest of the apartment," Elizabeth said, kicking off the sheet and sitting up cross-legged on the bed, her nightgown bunched up around her. If the aftermath of the party they'd had on Friday night was any indication, their apartment was going to be a total disaster zone. Elizabeth pictured a larger version of Jessica's room at home: clothes piled high, magazines and books everywhere, cosmetics covering any space that was left. Elizabeth could already feel her blood boiling. "Jessica, you can't keep the apartment such a mess all the time," she said sharply.

"Liz!" Jessica protested. "We haven't even moved in yet, and you're already complaining!"

Elizabeth had to laugh. "You're right," she admitted. "I guess I am being kind of uptight. It *will* be fun to have friends over to our own place."

"How do you think we should decorate the apartment?" Jessica wondered.

"I was thinking pastels," Elizabeth answered. "Soft colors—lilacs and mauves."

"Ugh," Jessica said, wrinkling her nose. "That sounds like some kind of boring nightmare. We've definitely got to do primaries—really cool, bold colors, like yellows and reds."

"That sounds like an overexciting nightmare," Elizabeth retorted. "Jessica, I really don't think you should be the one to make the decorating choices. If you remember, your room was chocolate-brown for years." In a moment of rebellion Jessica had decorated her entire room in shades of brown, from the carpeting to the walls. The twins had affectionately named it The Hershey Bar.

Both girls laughed. "That's no indication of my tastes," Jessica protested. "I was just trying to make a point."

"I think you made it," Elizabeth said. "None of us would dare venture in there."

"Hey, maybe Mom will do the apartment for us,"

Jessica said. "I bet most SVU students don't have their places decorated by an interior designer."

Elizabeth sighed, thinking about her mother. When the twins had called home earlier and got the answering machine, they were both pretty relieved. Elizabeth didn't think their parents would stand in the way of their higher education, but they might insist they were too young for college life. And they certainly wouldn't be pleased that the last of their children were leaving the nest. Elizabeth remembered how hard her mother had taken it when Steven had left for college. "My little boy," she had said, tears streaming down her face. "He's all grown-up." Even her father had had tears in his eyes.

In typical twin fashion Jessica's train of thought followed hers. "Do you think Mom and Dad will give us a hard time?" she wondered aloud.

"I don't know," Elizabeth admitted. "They have a pretty special way of laying on the guilt—thick."

"Well, that's never bothered me before," Jessica said.

That was certainly true, Elizabeth thought. Jessica never let anybody throw a guilt trip on her. She had been two-timing Ken all week and didn't even seem to give it a second thought. Not to mention lying to Zach about her age. And hiding Zach from Magda.

"Do you think they'll miss us?" Elizabeth asked softly.

"What do they need us for?" Jessica replied casually, flicking off the light. "They've got Prince Albert." Prince Albert was the Wakefields' golden Labrador.

Jessica lay down and curled up under the covers. "I'm going to sleep now," she said. "Night, Liz."

"Night," Elizabeth said, amazed at her sister's blasé attitude. How could Jessica always take everything so lightly? Elizabeth shook her head as she crawled under the blankets. She and Jessica really were like pastels and primaries. Unlike Jessica, Elizabeth felt responsible for everybody around her. She felt as if she were abandoning her boyfriend, her friends, and her parents. She stared up at the ceiling, watching the patterns change as car headlights illuminated the wall. Guilt weighed upon her like a ton of bricks.

Chapter 7

It was a misty, stormy day, and the ocean was an angry tumult of violent waves and whitecaps. Jessica stood alone at the edge of the sea, ankle-deep in water. Her blue-green eyes flashed with longing. The blue-green ocean flashed back, calling her out to the sea. Waves crashed against her ankles. Salt water sprayed into her mouth. Jessica took a few tentative steps forward.

"Jessica, c'mon!" Ken called, tugging at her arm.

Jessica looked behind her. The Sweet Valley High gang was playing volleyball in the sand.

"Over here, Jess!" Lila shouted, wearing hip-hugging shorts and a bikini top. She hit the ball over the net.

"C'mon, Jessica!" Winston yelled, waving a gangly arm. He got hit by the ball and stumbled.

"C'mon, Jessica, c'mon!" the gang called.

Just then Zach appeared from the water like a sea god and took her other arm. He looked strong and virile, and the entire ocean was reflected in his deep-green eyes.

"Come with me, Jess," Zach said, his voice low and seductive as he lead her out into the tempestuous sea. Jessica looked out at the vast expanse of water stretching to the horizon, and her stomach coiled in fear and excitement.

"Come with me," Zach repeated enticingly.

Come with me, come with me. The words swirled in Jessica's head. She opened her eyes, expecting to find an ocean in front of her. Where was she? Jessica sat up and blinked, trying to orient herself. She was in Steven and Billie's sofa bed. It was the crack of dawn on Thursday morning, and sun was streaming into the living room. The image of the stormy sea was so vivid in her mind that Jessica could almost smell the salt air. She rubbed her eyes, trying to clear her head of the vision of the ocean and the two handsome guys pulling both her arms.

I wonder if that qualifies as a good dream or a bad dream, Jessica mused. She had two guys pulling her in different directions. *Well, two guys are definitely a good thing,* she decided. *I think.*

Jessica drew her knees up to her chest and pondered the meaning of the dream. Ken was drawing her backward, toward the security of home, and Zach was pulling her forward, to the excitement of a new world. But why was Zach luring her out to sea? *What does that mean?* Jessica wondered. That she was in over her head? That she was drowning? Her stomach coiled in anticipation, as it had in her dream. She really was diving in headfirst to a brand-new world.

Jessica considered going back to sleep, to try to return to her dream. She wondered how it would end: Would she sink or swim?

Elizabeth flipped over groggily and opened her eyes, shielding them with her hand from the sunlight streaming through the window. "What time is it?" she mumbled, feeling for her alarm clock and knocking it off the side table. She groped for it on the floor and looked at the time. "Six A.M.," she groaned, bunching up her pillow and burrowing under the covers.

"I just had the weirdest dream," Jessica said.

"Mmm?" Elizabeth murmured sleepily.

"I was standing in the ocean looking out to sea, when Ken called to me. He was playing volleyball on the beach with Lila and Winston," Jessica recalled. Elizabeth peeked out of the covers, half listening as Jessica recounted her dream. "And then Zach appeared like a sea god from the water," Jessica said. "He was calling me out to the ocean, luring me with this sexy voice. I looked out at the horizon, feeling both scared and excited. And then I woke up."

"Maybe you feel torn between Zach and Ken," Elizabeth suggested.

"Thank you, Herr Freud," Jessica said sarcastically. "That part was easy to figure out."

Elizabeth laughed. "Can I help it if you have obvious dreams?"

"Hey, what's that sound?" Jessica said, sitting up suddenly.

Elizabeth frowned and listened. "It sounds like singing," she decided finally. They could hear Billie

95

and Steven's voices wafting gaily from the kitchen.

Jessica moaned and pulled the covers over her head. "Are they nuts?" she moaned. "At this hour of the morning?"

"It's the college girls!" Billie called, beaming as Jessica and Elizabeth sleepily entered the sunny kitchen.

"Huh?" Jessica mumbled. She ran a hand through her tangled hair, feeling bewildered. Why were Steven and Billie so full of energy at this hour of the morning? Was it somebody's birthday? Billie looked bright and cheery, wearing a loose-fitting green cotton dress that brought out highlights in her eyes. Her silky chestnut hair was tied back in a ribbon at the nape of her neck. Even their brother, who was usually such a grouch in the morning, seemed to be in particularly high spirits. He was clean shaven, and his hair was damp from a shower.

"We just heard the news!" Steven said, puffed up like a proud father.

"What news?" Elizabeth asked.

"That Jessica has decided to stay at SVU, too," Billie replied.

"But how did you find out?" Jessica asked, alarmed. She had told only Lila and Ken. How had the news got back to Steven and Billie so fast?

"Ken told us last night," Steven explained. "He called for you while you were out with Magda." Jessica had told Billie and Steven she was going to the movies with some of the Thetas. She had decided to confide in Billie about her dilemma with Zach and Magda, but Steven didn't know anything about it. He would hit the roof if he knew she was dating a college guy.

Jessica looked at Elizabeth worriedly. Did this mean their parents had heard as well? Had Steven called them?

"Don't worry, I don't think Mom and Dad know yet," Steven said, noting the look that passed between them. "But I'm sure they'll be thrilled when they find out!"

"Their two girls, all grown-up," Billie added.

Jessica stared at Elizabeth in consternation. Had Billie and Steven gone insane?

"Congratulations!" Steven called, pulling both twins toward him for a hug and kissing them both on the cheeks.

"Yuck," Jessica said, wiping her cheek. Elizabeth just looked at him warily.

"And to celebrate, we've prepared a 'Welcome to College Life' breakfast," Billie said, ushering the girls to the table. A bright-yellow tablecloth was draped over the round wooden table, and a display of high-energy health foods covered it.

Jessica's eyes almost popped out of her head as she took in the spread—wheat germ, oat-bran muffins, granola with yogurt and muesli, a tofu salad . . . Tofu? For breakfast? Where was the fresh-roasted coffee? Where were the chocolate-chip pancakes and blueberry muffins? Where were the fried eggs and sizzling strips of bacon?

"What are we supposed to do with this?" she whispered to Elizabeth, staring at the food in alarm.

"Jessica, we have to eat it!" Elizabeth hissed, picking up her napkin and folding it on her lap. "They went to all this trouble."

Jessica's eyes widened as Steven came to the table with a revolting-looking brown concoction in a big glass shake container. "What's that?" she asked nervously.

"This is the famous Steven Wakefield high-protein shake," he said, holding it aloft with a proud flourish. "My secret recipe of pureed bananas, mangoes, carrots, bean sprouts, and egg whites. And just a touch of honey." Jessica blanched as he listed the ingredients.

Steven smiled at the twins as he set the shake down on the table. "You have to drink these as often as possible," he said. "It's the only way to recover from the all-nighters you'll have to pull."

Jessica glanced at Elizabeth. Was he kidding? She would have thought so, but Billie was smiling and nodding. And Billie wasn't the type to joke about stuff like all-nighters.

"Steven's right," Billie agreed merrily, setting down two tall shake glasses in front of Jessica and Elizabeth and pouring the thick brown foaming liquid into them.

"Well, dig in," Billie said, sitting down at the table and filling her plate. "Here, Steven," she said, spooning some tofu salad onto his plate. "I made your favorite."

Steven speared a large chunk of tofu with his fork. "Mmm," he said, smacking his lips appreciatively. "Billie, you've really outdone yourself today. What did you put in the dressing this time? Chili powder?"

"Just a touch of ginger," Billie replied.

"Ahh, ginger," Steven said, nodding his head.

"Here, Jess, let me help you," Billie offered, picking up her empty plate.

Jessica watched in alarm as Billie loaded her plate with every item on the table. "Uh, I'm not really that hungry," she mumbled.

"Well, this way you can have a taste of everything," Billie said. "Here you are!" she said cheerily, handing her a heaping platter. Billie turned and started loading Elizabeth's plate.

"Hey, Jess, don't look so worried," Steven said reassuringly, slicing a banana into his bowl of wheat germ. "You don't have to pull an all-nighter every night."

"Of course not," Billie agreed, lifting a spoonful of muesli to her mouth. "It's not so bad—only three or four times a week."

Jessica's mouth dropped open. Three or four times a week! College was about sleeping late and meeting for lunch—not staying at the library all night. There was no way she was pulling any all-nighters. After all, she needed her beauty sleep.

Jessica pushed her food around her plate with her fork, looking for the least offensive item. She finally decided on an oat-bran muffin and reached into the basket in the middle of the table. *You could probably kill somebody with this,* she thought, weighing the muffin in her hand. She nibbled at it tentatively and wrinkled her nose. Disgusting! It tasted like gerbil food.

"Well, I better have some of this," Elizabeth said, picking up her shake glass. "I still haven't recovered from staying up all night to finish my essay for Professor Newkirk."

Elizabeth took a big gulp, then grimaced and almost choked. She ran to the sink and spit it out. "Uh, sorry," she said, turning to Billie and Steven. "I guess I'm not quite cut out for this yet."

"Oh, don't worry," Steven said magnanimously. "You'll get used to it."

"You'll have to," Billie added ominously.

"Have you heard about the plan?" Todd asked a group of cheerleaders in the cafeteria on Thursday. Todd, Ken, Lila, and Enid were rallying all their friends to caravan up to SVU Saturday and surprise the twins. They were going to put their reverse-psychology scheme into action.

"What plan?" Maria asked.

"Operation Get the Wakefield Twins back to Sweet Valley High," Todd said, his deep coffee-colored eyes twinkling with excitement. "We're going to take a road trip up to SVU on Saturday to surprise the twins."

"Well, I don't think we'll have any problems getting there," Amy said. "But how are we going to get them to come back?"

"Reverse psychology, that's how," Todd replied. "We're going to act so happy for the twins that they're going to regret their decision and come crawling back."

"That's a fabulous idea!" Sandy Bacon enthused. All the girls chorused their agreement except for one—Heather Mallone, the cocaptain of the cheerleading squad. She was sitting back from the group with her legs crossed, a dour expression on her face.

"If anybody's interested, we're meeting outside in fifteen minutes," Todd added, distributing colorful flyers with "Operation Wakefield Twins" marked on the front and directions to SVU on the back. "We're heading up to SVU on Saturday afternoon."

"Oh, how sweet," Heather murmured sarcastically, picking up a bright-blue flyer and looking at it with disdain. "There's just one little problem, Todd," she said, letting the flyer slip through her perfectly manicured fingers and fixing Todd with her steely blue eyes.

"What's that?" Todd asked, eyeing Heather warily. Ever since Heather had moved to Sweet Valley High, she and Jessica had been in open competition. Even though Heather and Jessica were cocaptains of the cheerleading squad, they acted more like archrivals. Heather would be thrilled if Jessica stayed at SVU, Todd thought worriedly. Then she would have the whole squad to herself.

"We've got cheerleading practice on Saturday afternoon," Heather continued. "Jessica obviously has no qualms about abandoning the squad, but for the rest of us, dedication is our number-one principle." She smiled sweetly at the group. "Oh, well, I guess we won't be able to join you on your little field trip, right, girls?" Amy's face fell, and Maria and Sandy looked crestfallen. Heather gathered together the flyers and handed them back to Todd.

Todd could feel his pulse quicken. There was no way he was going to let bossy Heather Mallone ruin the plan for her own selfish reasons. He looked at her angrily and opened his mouth to give her a piece of his mind. But then he shut it. He was not going to be the one to get into a tête-à-tête with Heather Mallone. This was a job for Lila. He would let her handle it.

"Well, why don't we just meet now and worry about the details later?" Todd said in a conciliatory tone, smiling calmly and dropping the flyers onto the table. He jumped up before Heather could protest further. As he made his way to Olivia's table, he could feel Heather's eyes boring angry holes in his back.

Fifteen minutes later a large group was gathered in a circle on the lawn. *Jessica and Elizabeth can certainly draw a crowd,* thought Todd with satisfaction as he looked around the group: Winston and Maria; Amy, Sandy, and Jean West from the cheerleading squad; Olivia Davidson and Penny Ayala from *The Oracle;* Annie Whitman and her stepsister, Cheryl Thomas. Even Bruce Patman had shown up. *And they're all psyched about the idea,* Todd thought happily. For the first time all week, he felt his spirits rising. Maybe this plan really would work.

"OK," Lila began, rubbing her hands together and smiling wickedly. "We've come up with a foolproof three-part reverse-psychology plan to get Jessica and Elizabeth back where they belong." A small cheer greeted her announcement.

"Each part of the plan corresponds to three basic human emotions," Ken explained. "Regret, jealousy, and pain." He picked up his turkey sandwich and took a big bite.

"Ouch!" Winston said. "You guys are really playing dirty."

"Desperation will lead a man to do many things, Winston," Ken replied.

"Part one," Lila said. "Regret. We're going to act really happy for the twins and cheerfully mention all the things they're leaving behind. For instance, their friends and family."

"And the cheerleading squad," Amy added.

"I know Jessica misses Heather," Maria joked. Everybody laughed.

"Mentioning Mr. Collins and *The Oracle* should work with Elizabeth, though," Olivia put in.

"Plus all their favorite hangouts," Winston said. "We can't forget the Dairi Burger, Casey's, Miller's Point—"

"Prince Albert," Bruce said with a scowl, drawing a general laugh.

"Hey, I know!" Olivia said. "Why don't we do this through illustrations? We can put together a photo collage and a slide show."

"That's a great idea!" Todd enthused. "We can use my slide projector."

"I'd love to help you put it together, Olivia," Penny Ayala, the editor in chief of *The Oracle,* offered. "I've got some great shots of Liz hard at work on her column."

"And I've got a few key cheerleading moments," Amy added.

"OK," Winston said. "So now we've succeeded in making the twins really sad. They've taken a trip down memory lane and regret leaving their lives behind. Now what?"

"Now it's time for the second part of the plan," Enid explained, taking over. "Envy. We're not only happy for them, we're happy for us. For instance, without Elizabeth around I'll be the smartest girl in school."

"And I'll be the star reporter for *The Oracle*," Olivia said, catching on.

"I'll be undisputedly the best-dressed and most popular girl at Sweet Valley High," Lila added.

"Hey, I'm not so sure about that!" Amy protested.

"OK," Winston said. "They're sad, they're green with envy, and then—"

"And then we let the final bomb drop," Ken said with satisfaction.

"Part three," Todd explained, his brown eyes gleaming. "Pain."

"Todd and I are going to tell the twins that we don't want to hold them back from their lives at SVU," Ken said.

"After all," Todd put in, "they shouldn't be tied down to high-school guys when they're in college."

"If that doesn't get them," Lila said with a sly grin, "nothing will!"

"Heather, I know you want our plan to fail so you really can be the sole captain of the cheerleading squad," Lila pointed out in frustration. She was trying to convince Heather to let the cheerleaders skip practice on Saturday and head to SVU. Heather was being belligerent as usual. Lila shook her head. She couldn't believe she had actually liked this girl once.

When Heather had first started at Sweet Valley High, she had created quite a stir. She was beautiful and talented and an exceptional cheerleader. She had been the captain of the squad at her old school, and she had enticed the Sweet Valley cheerleaders with a promise to lead them to Nationals. Everybody had fallen prey to her charm. Everyone except Jessica, that is. It wasn't until Heather took over the cheer-leading squad and kicked off two of the members that her real nature showed itself.

"Lila, how could you ever think such a thing?" Heather said, pretending to be shocked at Lila's state-ment. "You know how *integral* Jessie is to our team."

"Her name is Jessica!" Lila snapped, putting her hands on her hips. Lila knew that Jessica hated it when people called her Jessie—and whenever Heather called her by that nickname, Jessica went berserk.

"Oh, I know, but *Jessie* just seems to suit her," Heather said. "It goes along with her cute, bouncy personality."

Lila was getting fed up with Heather's act. "Heather, you are not going to accomplish anything by holding the girls back," she said, her brown eyes flashing. "The rest of us are going to go up to SVU whether or not you let them miss practice." She tapped a low heel impatiently.

"Look," Heather said, her tone darkening. "Just because the little Wakefield twinkies decide to play at being college women doesn't mean I have to give up my practice."

Lila gritted her teeth in frustration. "Heather, must you be such a dictator? Just because you don't like Jessica doesn't mean you should hold back the entire squad from helping one of our friends."

"Hey, Lila!" Todd called, running up to them.

"What?" Lila hissed between clenched teeth. Heather glared at him with narrowed eyes. Todd took a step back as he noticed the venom flying between them. "Did I interrupt something?" he asked.

"No, nothing at all," Heather said. "I was just leaving." She turned to go. "Oh, but I do want to be in your plan," she added, smiling sweetly. "Don't forget to let Jessica know that I'll take great pleasure in being the sole captain of the cheerleading squad." She paused. "I mean, reverse psychology, of course."

Lila rolled her eyes. "I'll be sure to tell her," she said wryly. "If anything will get Jessica running back here, it'll be that tidbit of information."

"Ta-ta!" Heather said, flitting away.

"Ta-ta," Lila muttered under her breath. "Well, it looks like we're going to get a late start on Saturday," she said, turning to Todd with a sigh.

"That's OK," Todd reassured her. "Otherwise, things are looking good. I talked to Mr. and Mrs. Wakefield last night, and they're in on the 'Get the Twins Back to Sweet Valley High' plan."

"I talked to Billie and Steven, and they're in on it, too," Lila informed Todd. "Only for them it's 'Operation Get the Twins out of SVU.' In fact, Steven's so desperate to get rid of his sisters that he said we could all crash at his apartment on Saturday." Lila paused for a moment. "I wonder if there'll be any hot parties that night," she said lightly.

Chapter 8

"Girls, I think it's a wonderful idea to stay at SVU!" Mrs. Wakefield enthused. Elizabeth almost dropped the phone, and she and Jessica looked at each other in shock. It was Thursday afternoon, and Jessica and Elizabeth had just summoned enough courage to break the news to their parents. Elizabeth was holding the phone and Jessica was right beside her, leaning in close to the receiver to hear.

Mrs. Wakefield laughed a light, girlish laugh. "You know, it's funny, but I feel so much younger with you two away, as if I'm not a mother anymore. It's kind of a relief not to have to worry about parental duties."

Elizabeth felt hurt. "But, Mom, don't you miss us?"

"Of course I do, darling," Mrs. Wakefield said warmly. "It's just that I think your father and I could use a break from parenting. Maybe we can even take that long trip to Europe we've always dreamed about."

Jessica and Elizabeth were speechless. "It's too bad

you won't get to live in a freshman dorm, though," her mother went on. "I always thought that was the best part of college. And, of course, you won't have a senior prom or a high-school graduation."

Elizabeth felt pangs of regret as her mother spoke, as if somebody else were stealing her life away. She had always dreamed of going to the prom with Todd. And of making a valedictorian speech at graduation.

On Thursday afternoon Ken sat at Lila's large mahogany kitchen table, sketching "Welcome to SVU" with colored markers on a huge banner. A heaping pile of colorful paper hats sat next to it on the table. Ken and Todd were making last-minute preparations with Enid and Lila at the Fowler mansion. Ken was fashioning party decorations, Lila and Todd were baking a cake, and Enid was making chocolate-chip-cookie squares.

Ken fumbled through the array of multicolored markers on the table and picked out a fuchsia one. He colored in the W absentmindedly, thinking about the twins' decision to stay at SVU.

He couldn't quite figure out why Jessica wanted to start college early. He could understand why Elizabeth wanted to stay. After all, she had the chance to get a job at a real newspaper and to work under the guidance of a world-renowned journalist. It was the opportunity of a lifetime.

But Jessica? What was Sweet Valley University offering her that Sweet Valley High didn't? Ken replayed in his mind his conversation with her. Jessica had talked about all the new possibilities open to her at college—sororities, cheerleading, plays. But those were the same things she did at high school. Jessica was an active member of Pi Beta Alpha, the most exclusive sorority at Sweet Valley High; she was cocaptain of the cheerleading squad; she had starred in the school's production of *Macbeth*. . . .

There must be more to it, Ken reasoned. What else had she told him? That she was staying to be with Elizabeth, that she couldn't abandon her twin. But that didn't sound like Jessica. She wouldn't drop her whole life just to keep Elizabeth company. Jessica had a lot of wonderful qualities, but selflessness wasn't one of them.

Ken shook his head and picked up a gold marker, sketching little stars around the border of the sign. Something bothered him about the whole situation. He just didn't know what it was.

Ken's ruminations were interrupted by sounds of bickering from the other side of the kitchen. Lila's shocked voice carried across the room. "A chocolate cake with whipped-cream frosting! You have got to be kidding!"

"Do you have a better suggestion?" came Todd's irritated response.

Even though they were all in the same room, the kitchen at Fowler Crest was so palatial that it could have been a suite of its own. Iron vats and copper kettles hung from the high ceiling, and a maid's chamber stood off a back entrance.

"Why don't we get Ken's opinion on the matter?"

Enid said in a conciliatory tone, coming over to the counter near Ken with a bowl of batter and a square cake pan. She hopped up on a stool and began stirring cookie dough with a big wooden spoon.

"I'm not getting involved," Ken said, holding his hands up in the air.

"How's it going, man?" Todd asked, carrying an assortment of pots and pans to the counter and dumping them with a large clatter.

"Great," Ken replied, infusing his voice with an enthusiasm he didn't feel. "I'm almost done here."

"Hey, nice," Enid said, rifling through the party hats that Ken had decorated. "Ken," she added, "you are a man of surprising talents." She pulled on a bright-purple hat covered with little yellow moons and hopped up on a stool. "Here, Todd," she said, picking out a turquoise hat with faces on it and placing it on his head.

"Well, that's appropriate," Lila told Todd as she set down vats of sugar and flour on the counter. "A dunce cap." She unfolded a stepladder and climbed up on it, searching through an assortment of cookbooks in the cupboard.

"Hey, Ken," Todd said, "the queen is insulting your design."

"No offense, Ken," Lila said hastily. "It has nothing to do with the artwork."

"Very funny," Todd retorted. He leaned over, picked out a pitch-black hat, and held it out to Lila. "Maybe you should wear this one. A witch's cap."

"I don't wear party hats," Lila said, waving a dismissive hand. "Aha!" she exclaimed suddenly, pulling out a baking cookbook and sitting down on the ladder. She laid the book on the counter and flipped through it. "There!" she said, pointing to a picture of an elaborate cake. "A triple-layer cheesecake with berries in the middle—blueberries, raspberries, and strawberries."

"It's just a college party," Todd scoffed. "Not a gourmet dinner."

"Oh, Todd, you are such a Philistine," Lila groaned.

"Oh, Lila, you are such a snob," Todd returned, imitating her lilting tones.

"C'mon, you guys, we're never going to get anything accomplished at this rate," Enid broke in. "Hey, hey!" she scolded, swatting away Todd's hand as he reached into the chocolate-chip-cookie dough. "No male paws in the batter!"

Enid pulled out a shiny copper penny and laid it on the table. "OK, chocolate or cheesecake," she said. "Flip for it."

"Heads," Lila said immediately.

Enid flipped the coin in the air and caught it, slapping it on her left hand. "Tails," she said, giving Lila an apologetic look.

Lila groaned and put her head in her hands. "An all-chocolate cake! That goes against all the rules of dessert!"

"Don't worry," Ken said. "They'll love it. Chocolate is Jessica's favorite."

Lila sighed and began pulling out ingredients from the cabinet.

111

"So what's the update?" Todd asked the group.

"Well, Elizabeth sounded distinctly bummed when I asked her if I could take over her 'Personal Profiles' column on *The Oracle*," Enid said with a giggle. "I really laid it on thick. She could barely talk by the time we got through."

Lila laughed. "Jessica was exactly the same. She wasn't too pleased when I told her that I was going to be at the top of the social ladder without her. And she almost exploded when she remembered that Heather would be the sole captain of the cheerleading squad."

"Looks like everything's going according to plan," Todd said, rubbing his hands together. "I talked to Liz last night, and she was shocked by my sudden change in attitude." Todd looked over at Ken. "How about you? Did you get in touch with Jessica?"

"Yeah," Ken replied. "She was really bewildered, too. She couldn't understand why I was so happy for her all of a sudden."

Actually, Jessica hadn't even seemed to notice his change in attitude, Ken recalled, feeling worried inside. She had sounded distant and preoccupied, and she had been in a hurry to get off the phone. And unlike what Elizabeth had said to Todd, Jessica hadn't mentioned anything about weekend visits. Ken couldn't get rid of a nagging feeling that there was more to Jessica's story than just wanting to stay at college. But what was it? Had she met someone else?

"Hey, what's this?" Todd protested as Enid stuck her index finger into the cookie bowl and put a gob of chocolate-chip batter in her mouth.

"She said no *male* paws in the batter," Lila reminded Todd with a smile, joining Enid and dipping her finger into the bowl.

"Women!" Todd groaned, putting his head in his hands. "Ken, could you help me out here?" he pleaded. "I'm outnumbered."

Ken gave Todd a vacant stare. He had listened to the exchange halfheartedly, trying to seem as excited as the rest of them. But he was too caught up in his private thoughts to summon the energy to take part in their bantering.

"Hey, Ken, you there?" Todd asked, waving a hand in front of his face.

"Huh?" Ken asked, forcing a smile. "Oh, sure."

"Men!" Lila said, and she and Enid giggled together.

"Good morning, Mr. Petherbrook," Elizabeth said in a clipped, professional tone as she entered his office punctually at eight forty-five on Friday morning. On Wednesday he had told her she should try putting in a full day to see if she could handle it. Actually, "cut the mustard" was the expression he had used.

Mr. Petherbrook looked up from a sea of papers and fumbled for his glasses. "Good morning, er, uh—"

"Elizabeth," she supplied, taking a seat and clenching her bag tightly in her lap. Mr. Petherbrook pushed his glasses up on his nose, his eyes traveling slowly down her body. "Nice dress," he said, his gaze resting on her legs.

Elizabeth could feel the blood rush to her face.

She wasn't wearing a dress. She was wearing a conservative navy-blue suit with a cream silk blouse and low ivory pumps. She had borrowed the outfit from Billie, hoping to garner some respect with her professional attire. But it obviously didn't matter. Mr. Petherbrook would see her as a sex object no matter what she wore.

"Why don't you take a seat at my secretary's desk while I find something for you to do today?" Mr. Petherbrook suggested. "Annie's gone for the week. We were supposed to get a new girl, but she hasn't shown up." He scowled and picked up his cigar, making a round O with his lips as he lit it. "Can't get good help these days," he muttered, taking a few vigorous puffs. "Always the same thing with these girls at the temp agency."

Women! Elizabeth wanted to scream, but she controlled herself and stood up stiffly, careful to keep her hips from swaying as she walked into the outer chamber.

Five minutes later Elizabeth was still waiting. She drummed her fingers on the table impatiently. Suddenly the phone jangled and Elizabeth jumped. She looked at it with uncertainty. Should she answer it?

"Would you mind picking that up, dolly?" Mr. Petherbrook hollered from his office.

Elizabeth took a deep breath. "Cliff Petherbrook's office," she said. She scribbled down the message on a pink notepad and placed it on the desk. The moment the clock struck nine, the phone began ringing off the hook. As soon as Elizabeth would answer one call, another line would buzz. After ten minutes she wanted to pull her hair out. She was desperately trying to keep track of the people on hold, but she kept accidentally cutting them off.

Now I know what it feels like to be a secretary, Elizabeth thought half an hour later, running a hand through her disheveled hair.

Just then Mr. Petherbrook walked out of his office. Elizabeth handed him a stack of messages. "Thanks, sugar bun," he said, rifling through them.

"My name is Elizabeth," she said tightly.

"Ehh?" Mr. Petherbrook mumbled, distracted. He picked out a few messages and dropped the rest on her desk, heading back for his office.

"Mr. Petherbrook!" Elizabeth called sharply, gathering together the slips of pink paper that were cascading across her desk. He turned and looked at her impatiently. "Could you please give me my assignment for the day?" she asked.

"Oh, yes, right, your assignment," he said, pensive for a moment. "As it happens, I've got a load of work for you today."

Elizabeth's heart soared as he walked into his office. A load of work. She was going to get a real assignment. Maybe she was going to be able to do some investigative work on a story. Or make some important phone calls. Or fact-check an article. Or—

Suddenly the ringing of the phone cut into her reverie. Elizabeth sighed. "Cliff Petherbrook's office," she said into the receiver.

Mr. Petherbrook walked out with a thick stack of papers under his arms. Elizabeth's eyes lit up.

"Here you are," he said, dumping the pile onto the desk. He fished through a desk drawer and pulled out four boxes of office envelopes. "Now, we've got to have all of these stuffed by the end of the day."

Elizabeth's eyes almost popped out of her head. He wanted her to stuff envelopes!

"What's wrong? You don't think you can handle it, sugar?" Mr. Petherbrook asked.

"I think I can manage," Elizabeth replied stiffly.

"Fold, stuff, seal," he said. Then he laughed and patted her on the shoulder. "Don't worry, you'll get the hang of it in no time." He picked up his new messages and went back into his office.

"Fold, stuff, seal," muttered Elizabeth under her breath, picking up the first sheet of paper and examining it. It was a questionnaire regarding environmental practices in the workplace. Elizabeth creased the letter three times, stuffed it in an envelope, and licked the seal. "Fold, stuff, seal."

Elizabeth ran her thumb through the dense stack of papers. *There must be a thousand letters here,* she thought despairingly. It would take her hours to get through them. She wondered if she should just refuse to do the work. After all, she was an intern, not a secretary. Maybe she should march into Petherbrook's office and demand a real assignment. She hadn't worked so hard to get her journalism experience just to stuff envelopes.

But then Ian's advice came back to her. "You've got to fight your way to the top," he had said. "You can't just expect to get respect for nothing—you've got to *earn* it." *Ian was right*, Elizabeth thought, licking an envelope and dropping it into the box. She couldn't expect to waltz into the office and get top-notch assignments her first week there. She had to work her way up like everybody else.

By lunchtime, Elizabeth's stomach was growling and her nerves were shot. Her arms were aching and her lips tasted like sticky candy. Her head was ringing along with the ringing of the phones, and mindless words were echoing in succession in her head: *fold stuff seal, Mr. Petherbrook's office, you've got to earn respect.*

Elizabeth looked at the box in despair. No matter how many envelopes she stuffed, the pile didn't seem to get any smaller. Suddenly the phone jangled.

"Fold, stuff, seal," Elizabeth answered brightly. *Oh no*, she thought, dropping the phone with a clang and burying her head in her hands. *I'm losing my mind.*

Mr. Petherbrook emerged from his office at noon, a jacket thrown over his arm. "I'm just going out for a quick bite. You can handle it here without me, can't you?"

Elizabeth's eyes widened. Did that mean she wasn't going to get to eat lunch? "Don't worry," he said, clapping her on the back. "You're doing a great job, babe."

"Elizabeth, Elizabeth," she muttered through clenched teeth. The phone rang. "Mr. Petherbrook's office," she said. *Maybe this place will get better after lunch*, Elizabeth thought with a sigh. After all, it couldn't get worse.

117

But it did get worse. "Would you mind bringing me my messages, doll face?" Mr. Petherbrook asked when he got back. "I'm expecting an important call." Elizabeth spent the afternoon running in and out of his office, trying to keep up with the calls while she made copies and sent faxes. The phone switchboard was complicated and confusing, and Mr. Petherbrook kept barking out orders, making her job almost impossible. "You've got to earn respect," she kept saying to herself, working to the rhythm of the repetition of Ian's words.

"Hey, doll, do you think you can send a fax for me?" Mr. Petherbrook bellowed.

Elizabeth was reaching the boiling point. "Elizabeth," she said, marching into his office and grabbing the fax out of his hand. "My name is Elizabeth."

Mr. Petherbrook looked at her sympathetically. "Is the pressure getting to you, dearie?"

Elizabeth thought she was going to explode. She pivoted on her heel and marched out of the office. "*Is the pressure getting to you?*" she repeated, outraged. *I'm nothing more than Petherbrook's personal secretary,* she thought as she stomped into the copy room. *Personal slave is more like it,* she said to herself bitterly.

Elizabeth aggressively punched in the phone number on the fax machine and stuffed the page into the slot, waiting impatiently for the line to connect. She took long, haggard breaths trying to calm herself. She reminded herself that she was in the real world now. She couldn't expect all of her mentors to be as wonderful and helpful as Mr. Collins at *The Oracle*.

Mr. Petherbrook was slouched over her desk when she got back. "I thought you were answering the phones, doll face," he said, a scowl spreading across his loose jowls. "We just lost an important connection to London." He turned and walked out.

Elizabeth's eyes flashed. "I was trying to send this fax like you asked me to," she said angrily, waving it violently in the air as she followed him into his office.

Mr. Petherbrook sat down in the leather chair behind his big oak desk, rolling it around on the floor with his feet. "Sweetheart, sweetheart, this isn't high school anymore," he said as if he were speaking to an infant. "This is a real newsroom, with real pressure. If you want to make it in this world, you've got to learn to juggle your tasks."

Elizabeth stared at him, dumbfounded. Did he think she was an octopus? Or that her arms could stretch from the copy room to the office? *Juggle my tasks!* she fumed inwardly. She was tempted to pick up the typewriter and phone and start juggling them.

"So did you manage to send the fax, at least?" he asked, reaching out an arm to take it from her.

"The line was busy," Elizabeth said through clenched teeth.

Mr. Petherbrook leaned back in his chair and folded his arms across his chest. "Can't you do anything, doll face?" he asked, shaking his head and looking at her with a leer. "Or do you just stand there looking good?"

Elizabeth exploded. "First of all," she said, her

119

voice strong and determined. "My name is Elizabeth. Not 'doll face,' not 'sugar bun,' not 'honeybunch,' not 'sweetheart.'" She slammed the fax down on his desk with such violence that coffee sloshed out of his mug. "Secondly, I am an intern, not a personal slave. I will not get your coffee. I will not answer your phones. I will not send your faxes. I will not copy your personal papers."

Mr. Petherbrook shifted in his seat uncomfortably. Both doors were opened, and a crowd was beginning to gather in the hall. "Hey, keep your voice down," he said.

Elizabeth ignored him. "Thirdly, I will not be discriminated against on the grounds of my gender," she continued, her voice ringing out. People began whispering among themselves in the hall.

Mr. Petherbrook raised a hand and gave her an engaging smile. "Look, Ms. . . . er, Elizabeth. Calm down. Don't you think you're overreacting a bit?"

"Wakefield, Elizabeth Wakefield," she told him. "And no, I do not think I am overreacting." Elizabeth took a deep breath, forcing her voice to remain calm. "I don't know what year you think this is, but you're living in the past. This is a professional newsroom, and I expect professional treatment. Women are to be treated as equals, with respect and dignity." Elizabeth paused and a hushed silence filled the air. "Let me be the first to inform you that sexual harassment is no longer the norm, but a crime."

Mr. Petherbrook's eyes narrowed to tiny slits. "Is that a threat, Ms. Wakefield?"

"You can take it however you like, *Mr.* Petherbrook," Elizabeth said, gathering her coat and bag. A murmur rose from the crowd. "But for the moment you'll have to call one of your *girls* from the temp agency," she said. "Because I quit!"

Elizabeth walked out of the office with dignity, holding her head high. "Excuse me," she said tersely to the people gathered outside the office.

Well, I may have lost a job, but I guess I'm earning respect, she thought as she hurried out of the *Chronicle* office, already formulating her next story on sexual harassment in the workplace.

Chapter 9

"Hey, Steven, how are you doing?" a big, burly guy asked at the football field on Friday night. A golden Labrador was panting by his side, a rolled-up newspaper in her mouth.

"Marcus! Good to see you," Steven said, clapping him on the back.

The Labrador leaped up and threw a pair of excited paws on Billie's chest, tackling her to the ground. "Whoa!" Billie said with a laugh, rolling around on the grass with the dog. She knelt down and buried her face in the thick fur around the dog's neck. "How're you doing, Goldie?" The dog whined happily, answering Billie with a long, wet lick on the cheek.

Jessica sighed. She and Elizabeth were with Billie and Steven at the big game of the season against State. State was Sweet Valley University's number-one competitor, and the stands were packed to overflowing with enthusiastic fans. It looked as if there were a million people at the game, and Steven and Billie seemed to know all of them. They'd been trying to get to their seats for the last half hour, but every two minutes somebody else stopped them.

Jessica tapped her foot restlessly and took in the surroundings, looking around for someone she knew. The SVU band was setting up near the goal post, and the football players were in a huddle in the middle of the field with the coach. The SVU cheerleaders were revving up the fans, jumping around and shouting out cheers. The audience was responding spiritedly, waving banners and throwing confetti.

"Marcus, these are my little sisters, Jessica and Elizabeth," Steven said. "They're visiting for the week."

"Hey! Twins!" Marcus said, holding out a hand. "Twice as nice, huh?" he said to Steven with a grin.

"I wouldn't say that, exactly," Steven said with a wry smile.

"Steven!" Elizabeth protested, giving him a light punch. Then she turned to Marcus. "Nice to meet you," she said, shaking his hand and giving him a friendly smile.

Jessica just grunted and looked away. Steven kept introducing them as his "little sisters." It was so aggravating. Not to mention risky. What if one of Zach's fraternity brothers came up to them? Or Zach himself?

"So are you getting a feel for the big college life?" Marcus asked with a broad smile.

"It's really exciting," Elizabeth told him. "There's just so much to do here. It seems like there's a different cultural activity at the student union every night."

Jessica felt like vomiting. *Twice as nice. The big college life.* Didn't Elizabeth realize how condescending these people were? "I hope your big brother's keeping an eye on you," a shaggy-haired guy named Martin had said with a wink. "Isn't college wild and crazy?" a tall, geeky guy with dark glasses had said. "Oh, I remember when I was in high school!" a girl with frizzy red-blond hair had reminisced.

Jessica fidgeted impatiently and looked around for Zach. She had been scouting the field for him ever since they had arrived, but he was nowhere to be seen. Jessica yawned. It looked as if they were never going to sit down. Steven and Elizabeth were absorbed in a conversation with Marcus, and Billie was playing with Goldie.

"Here, Goldie!" Billie called, wresting a newspaper out of the dog's mouth and flinging it across the lawn. "Go get it!" The dog lunged for the paper and retrieved it, trotting back to Billie proudly, her tail held high.

"Hey, you guys," Jessica interrupted finally. "I think we should get to our seats. It looks like the game is about to start."

"Jessica's right," Steven said, clasping Marcus's hand. "Good seeing you, man!"

"C'mon, girls," Billie said with a smile, taking Jessica's and Elizabeth's arms. "Let's go find our seats. I think Steven wanted to get us all something to drink, didn't he?" She turned to look at Steven, her eyes twinkling.

"See you in ten minutes," Steven said with a sigh, heading off in the direction of the concession stand.

Finally, Jessica thought. But they hadn't walked more than ten feet before Billie was assaulted by a group of intellectual-looking students.

"Billie Winkler!" an artistic-looking woman with fair skin and a mass of curly red hair called. "Where have you been?"

"We've been looking all over for you," a bald man with an earring said.

Jessica stood back from the group, feeling lost. She had been so excited to go to a college football game. It was her first real SVU event. She had envisioned herself waltzing across the field, grabbing the attention of all the football players. But instead she was practically invisible. She was just Steven and Billie's little tagalong.

"We missed you at our philosophy discussion group on Sunday," the red-haired woman told Billie.

"I was otherwise occupied," Billie replied, giving the twins a wink. They had spent the whole day Sunday cleaning up the disaster caused by Jessica's party.

"These are Steven's sisters," Billie said, introducing them. "They're visiting from high school."

"Getting a feel for the big college life?" the red-haired woman said with a huge smile.

Jessica almost screamed.

❖   ❖   ❖

"Go, Vanguards!" the SVU fans yelled, rising to their feet spontaneously after an exciting last play right before halftime. The band struck up a chord, and multicolored confetti streamed down the stands in a parade of colors.

"Wildman Watts, he's our man!" the fans shouted. A touchdown in the last second by Tom Watts, the Vanguard quarterback, had brought the SVU team into the lead by one point. Jessica was pulled to her feet with the rest of the students, but she wasn't sharing their enthusiasm. Even though it was an action-packed game, with complicated plays and closely matched opponents, Jessica was bored. She didn't know any of the players, and she didn't feel any affinity for the Vanguards. Everybody was screaming about the phenomenal touchdown by the quarterback, but Jessica had no interest in him whatsoever.

Tom Watts had shone during the first half of the game. Every time she looked, the quarterback had the ball in his hand, dodging his opponents. But in her mind all Jessica saw was Ken. He looked so cute in his football uniform—particularly after a game when he was wearing jeans and his football shirt, his hair wet from a shower and his football helmet under his arm.

Being a part of things makes all the difference, Jessica mused, sitting down and picking up her drink. She took a long sip of lemonade and set it beside her. If it had been Ken that had made the final touchdown before halftime, she would have been yelling her lungs out at the sidelines, bursting with excitement as she led the cheerleaders onto the field.

Being at this game had made Jessica realize that she wasn't really interested in football. Half the fun was watching Ken play. The other half was cheerleading. *Football's about getting attention and talking to friends,* Jessica thought, *not about watching some unknown players beat some unknown team.*

The school song boomed from the loudspeakers, and the SVU cheerleaders trotted to the sidelines, wearing hip purple-and-gold outfits. Wild hooting and hollering greeted their appearance.

The head cheerleader ran to the middle of the field and did a double herky followed by a triple back flip and landed in a full split. *Wow,* Jessica thought, *that was amazing.* Her mouth dropped open as all the other cheerleaders followed with the same move in quick succession, ending in a V-for-Vanguards formation. The fans went wild, clapping in tune to the beat and shouting out the words of the school song.

The music segued into a funky rap beat, and the cheerleaders broke into a jazzy dance routine. Stomping their feet and swinging their hips, they twisted and turned and pranced and leaped. Jessica looked on in awe as they topped one move with another: one-armed cartwheels, double herkies, triple herkies, back handovers, front flips, line splits. Their movements were smooth and fluid, and they moved as a unit in perfect synchrony.

Jessica was stunned with the quality of the performance. She had thought the Sweet Valley High cheerleaders were good, but they looked like amateurs compared to the SVU squad. Last season she and

Heather had taken their team to Nationals, and they had placed second. Jessica had been thrilled to be ranked among the best in the nation. But this was a different league altogether. Jessica watched the captain of the squad as she flipped across the field and climbed to the top of a pyramid, holding her arms in an *L* formation. She had more than talent, Jessica decided. She had style. *Could I ever be that good?* she wondered.

Suddenly Jessica's excitement returned. She could see herself out on the field, flipping and turning with the other cheerleaders as the fans yelled their support. Once she joined the cheerleading squad, she would feel as if she belonged at SVU.

Billie turned to Jessica. "Aren't they great?" she asked.

"They're amazing," Jessica breathed.

"I think this squad is one of the best in the country," Billie said. "They're going to Nationals this year."

"I can't wait to be on the team!" Jessica said. Then she paused, feeling insecure. "But I wonder if I could make it. They've got cheerleading down to a science."

"Of course you could," Billie said encouragingly.

Jessica's eyes lit up. "Do you really think so?"

"Well, you'll have plenty of time to practice," Billie said. "This squad was picked months ago. You won't even be eligible to try out until next fall."

Jessica's heart sank. Cheerleading was such an important part of her life. She couldn't imagine a whole year without it. *And I'll miss cheering for Ken, too,* Jessica thought sadly.

*　　　　*　　　　*

"That's a really great outfit, Liz!" Jessica told her twin as they stood in a long line for hot dogs at half-time.

"Jessica, what are you talking about?" Elizabeth asked suspiciously. She was wearing faded jeans and a button-down blue cotton shirt with a ribbed ivory T-shirt underneath.

"You look really hip," Jessica said. "I like the leather belt with your jeans. And the blue shirt is pretty with your eyes."

Elizabeth glanced at her sister warily. Normally, Jessica would tell her that she should stop wearing old jeans and start paying attention to her appearance. Just yesterday Jessica had said she was embarrassed to be seen with her because she was wearing a peasant skirt and a gauze top. She didn't want the Theta sisters to think Elizabeth was a "granola type," she had said. Jessica was definitely up to something. And Elizabeth was in no mood for it. Her spirits were low, and her head was pounding. After her harrowing day at *The Chronicle,* the last thing she needed was Jessica's scheming.

"Hey, cute pendant," Jessica said, fingering the sparkling oval crystal hanging on a long black cord around Elizabeth's neck.

Elizabeth swatted her hand away. "Jessica, just tell me what you want," she snapped.

Jessica took a step back, her blue-green eyes wide. "Well, I see we've had a complete personality transformation," she said, sounding offended.

Elizabeth sighed. "I'm sorry," she said softly. "I'm

just in a bad mood, OK?" She pressed her fingers to her throbbing temples. "I quit *The Chronicle* today."

"You did what?" Jessica exclaimed.

"I quit," Elizabeth said with a sigh. "I walked out." She snapped her fingers in the air. "My internship is kaput, *finito*, done with, over, and gone."

"Oh, no," Jessica said. "Don't tell me you turned the tables on Featherhook."

Elizabeth had to laugh. Over the past two days Jessica had called her boss everything from Tetherhook to Bletherbrook to Leatherlook. "Something like that," she said, and she gave Jessica an abridged version of the day's events. Jessica's expression changed from sympathy to outrage to amusement as Elizabeth recounted her tale. She was laughing by the time Elizabeth finished.

"Liz, I've gotta hand it to you," Jessica said. "You certainly put him in his place, *dolly.*"

"I guess I did," Elizabeth replied. She couldn't help laughing along with her sister. But then her expression immediately sobered, and she sighed. "Now I've blown the whole internship." *What have I done?* Elizabeth thought in dismay. Not only had she ruined her chances for a position at the *Chronicle,* but she had cut off the possibility of working with Felicia Newkirk as well. After all, Professor Newkirk had landed this internship for her. She wouldn't be too pleased to hear that Elizabeth had just walked out after two days.

"Well, I've got an idea that might cheer you up," Jessica said brightly.

131

Elizabeth was immediately suspicious. *Here it comes,* she thought. She crossed her arms and listened with narrowed eyes while Jessica outlined her scheme for the Zeta formal. She wanted Elizabeth to pose as Jessica and double-date with Magda, leaving the real Jessica free to go to the dance with Zach. Since Elizabeth had no idea Magda was interested in Zach, Magda couldn't really hold it against her.

"So I'll go as you to the Zeta formal with Zach, and you'll go as me with Magda!" Jessica finished brightly. "Actually, we won't really be switching. I'll still be me, but I'll be wearing my hair like you usually do. And you'll also be me." She paused, looking pleased with herself. "Two Jessicas! Brilliant, isn't it?"

"Two Jessicas!" Elizabeth echoed, her mouth agape. "Don't you think one Jessica in the world is enough?"

"It's just for one night," Jessica said. "Just think, you can let your hair down for a change—literally."

"Jess, I have no desire to let my hair down," Elizabeth said hotly, flipping her ponytail as she spoke. "Furthermore, I have absolutely no interest in this Theta-Zeta affair."

Elizabeth couldn't believe her sister's gall. First Jessica had manipulated her into throwing a party behind Steven's back, and now Jessica wanted her to pose as Jessica at some horrible fraternity event. Elizabeth was fed up. Her life was already a mess. There was no way her twin was going to get her involved in another disastrous scheme.

"Oh, Lizzie, c'mon," Jessica cajoled. "It'll be fun.

Our first real college affair. You'll get to meet all the Theta sisters and—"

Elizabeth cut her off. "Jessica, read my lips," she said sternly. "No way."

"But, Liz—" Jessica protested.

"Hey, how's my favorite journalist?" a familiar male voice interrupted from behind them.

Elizabeth spun around. Ian Cooke stood there, holding a soda in his hand.

"Ian!" Elizabeth exclaimed, greeting him like a long-lost friend. "I was hoping you would turn up," she said, feeling more pleased to see him than she had expected she would. "Why don't you join us in line?"

Elizabeth hooked her arm through his and turned her back on her glowering sister. *Jessica doesn't know when to stop,* she thought. *Her plan is a fiasco just waiting to happen!*

Chapter 10

"Hey, Todd, do you have the slide projector?" Ken yelled from the doorway of the Wilkinses' house on Saturday afternoon. "I can't find it anywhere."

"I've got it!" Todd shouted back, ducking into the backseat of his BMW and placing the slide projector securely on the seat. Todd was wound up with excitement. Everything depended on the party tonight, and he didn't want anything to go wrong. *What if Olivia forgets the slides?* he worried. *Or if the girls can't get out of cheerleading practice in time to come with us?* Todd glanced at his watch, impatient to get on the road. They were planning to leave as soon as Amy, Maria, and Sandy were free from Heather's clutches.

Suddenly Prince Albert started yapping excitedly and biting at Todd's heels. They had decided to bring him along to pay his last respects. Todd laughed and bent down to pet the Wakefields' golden Labrador. "I guess you're excited too, huh, boy?"

"Arf!" Prince Albert agreed, wagging his tail wildly.

Ken emerged from the doorway, his face hidden behind a heaping mass of party paraphernalia. His arms were piled high with streamers and party hats, and a long, flowing banner was draped over his left shoulder. Ken staggered to the car, and Todd jumped to open the door for him.

"Phew," Ken said after he unloaded the pile into the backseat of the car. "I never realized paper products could be so unwieldy."

Just then a car came honking down Country Club Drive, the engine churning and sputtering. It was Winston, Enid, and Olivia in Winston's beat-up orange Volkswagen bug.

"Road trip!" Winston yelled, pressing his hand down on the horn.

"SVU, here we come!" Olivia and Enid shouted, hanging out the windows and waving excitedly.

"Hi, guys!" Todd called as they clambered out of the car. "Hey, Winston, quit that honking. Are you trying to wake all the neighbors?"

"Do you think they're sleeping at this hour of the day?" Winston asked. Winston was wearing a goofy cap with a big yellow plastic sunflower on it.

"Here, Todd, have a whiff," Winston suggested, bowing his head to display the flower. Without thinking Todd pulled down the stem of the flower and leaned in to smell it. A burst of cold water squirted into his face.

Todd spluttered and backed away. "Winston," Todd said dangerously, wiping off his face with the back of his sleeve, "sometimes I can't believe I'm friends with you."

"I've got the slides," Olivia said, patting her bag as she joined them. Her curly brown hair was tucked into a turquoise bandanna, and her hazel eyes were bright with excitement.

Todd breathed a sigh of relief. "That's great," he said. "I'm so glad you and Penny put them together."

"What, no time to stop and smell the flowers?" Winston joked to Olivia, an expression of mock hurt on his face.

"Winston, you're such a goof," Olivia said. "Only an idiot would fall for that old trick."

Winston laughed. "Todd, I think you've just been insulted."

Olivia clapped her hand to her mouth. "Todd, you didn't?" she exclaimed, giggling. Then she noticed that Todd's face was dripping wet. "You did!"

"Would you give me those slides?" he ordered, glowering at both of them.

A moment later Lila pulled up in her lime-green Triumph. She steered her car expertly into the Wilkinses' round driveway and hopped out, looking chic in a black linen suit.

"Hello all," Lila said, pushing her sunglasses up onto her head. "Nice hat, Winston," she murmured, raising an eyebrow.

"Thanks, Lila," Winston said. "I got it at Lisette's. It's the latest this season—and it was on sale."

"Lila, we're going to a college campus, you know,"

Todd snorted, taking in her outfit, "not a debutante ball."

"Well, I hope they let you in," Lila retorted. "I don't think scruffy little children are allowed on the campus."

Ken and Enid looked at each other. "Just can't take them anywhere," Ken said, shaking his head.

"Let's get this show on the road!" Winston called, rubbing his hands together. "What are we waiting for?"

"Maria—your girlfriend—for one," Todd said. "And Amy and Sandy."

"Oh, right," Winston said sheepishly. "They're at the mercy of the evil Heather Mallone."

"Well, why don't we do a quick run-through of the plan while we're waiting?" Ken suggested.

"It can't hurt," Olivia said, hopping up on the bumper of Winston's car.

"Now, assuming that Heather hasn't taken the cheerleading squad hostage, we should get to the campus around seven o'clock," Ken said, jumping up to join Olivia.

The Volkswagen sank a few inches, wheezing in protest. Winston moaned. "My baby!" he yelled, putting his arms around the hood.

"Now, now," Olivia consoled Winston, patting him on the head. Then she turned her attention to Ken. "How are we going to set up with the twins there?" she asked.

"Billie told me that they were invited to some frat thing, so we can prepare our surprise going-away party while they're out," Todd explained, leaning against his BMW.

"As soon as they get home, Billie and Steven are going to start a mock episode of *This is Your Life* with the twins on the slide projector," Ken said.

"And then each of us will narrate one of the episodes," Todd added.

Lila took over, her brown eyes glinting. "And then after they're sufficiently sad, we'll shift into part two of the plan—envy."

"We'll break up into a normal party, but each of us will try to get our digs in," Enid said.

"And if that still doesn't work," Lila continued, "then Todd and Ken will drop the final bomb."

"So what do you think?" Todd asked, looking around the group anxiously.

"It's a great plan," Winston said. "I'm glad I thought of it," he joked.

"It's got to work," Enid added.

"It's foolproof," Olivia put in confidently.

"Arf!" Prince Albert barked, jumping around excitedly.

"I guess Prince Albert thinks so, too," Todd laughed. He grabbed the dog's leash and led him into the car.

"Elizabeth, will you look at this?" Jessica breathed, holding up a gorgeous rose-colored mid-calf-length ball gown to Elizabeth. "It's got you written all over it. And it would be perfect for the Zeta dinner."

Jessica and Elizabeth were at an exclusive shop in town on Saturday afternoon, hunting for a formal dress for Jessica. Elizabeth had wanted to go to the student union to check out the cultural events of the day, but Jessica convinced her to accompany her shopping.

"It would be perfect," Elizabeth agreed, fingering the delicate material. "Except for one tiny detail."

Jessica held her breath. "What's that?" she said hopefully.

"I'm not going to the Zeta dinner," Elizabeth said. But she couldn't resist holding the dress against her and taking a quick look in the mirror. It had a square-cut bodice with lace trim that narrowed into a slim waist and flowed out gracefully into a full skirt. The dress really was perfect for her.

"Oh, that detail," Jessica said, her face darkening with disappointment.

Elizabeth put the dress back on the rack and wandered away.

"Oh, well, forget it, no big deal," Jessica muttered, following her. "I'll just go to the dance with Zach by myself and be blackballed forever from the Thetas. And sacrifice my entire future at SVU." She sighed dramatically and headed for the evening-wear section.

Elizabeth rolled her eyes. "Jessica, that's not going to work. You don't *have* to go to the dance with Zach."

"But I already told him I was going," Jessica explained, rifling through a rack of skimpy black dresses.

"I guess you'll just have to tell him you changed your mind," Elizabeth said flatly.

Jessica picked up a form-fitting crushed-velvet minihalter dress and held it against her body. "Hey, Liz," Jessica said lightly.

140

"What?" Elizabeth asked, her tone wary.

"Remember the week that Todd lived at our house when Mom and Dad were away and I covered for you?" Elizabeth sighed and didn't answer. She knew there was more coming.

"And remember how Magda invited us for a tour of the Theta House on Monday and you didn't show?" Jessica reminded her twin. "And how I made up a story that you were auditioning for the new student TV station?"

Elizabeth crossed her arms over her chest.

"And then the Thetas invited us for lunch on Tuesday," Jessica went on. "And I went out of my way to explain that you were unreachable because you were already on campus."

Elizabeth could feel herself softening. She had no desire to rush the Thetas, but Jessica had been covering for her all week. "Jessica, what's your point?" she asked, trying to keep an impassive look on her face.

"Lizzie, can't you please, please do this tiny thing for me?" Jessica begged. "We're twins, we have to stick by one another—through thick or thin."

"All right, all right," Elizabeth growled, grabbing the rose-colored dress off the rack. "But on one condition."

"Name it," Jessica said breathlessly.

"This one's on you," Elizabeth said, throwing the dress into Jessica's arms.

"No problem," Jessica agreed. She grabbed the halter dress off the rack and flipped open her wallet, pulling out the "emergency" credit card Mr. Wakefield had given them. "If needing two dresses isn't an emergency," Jessica proclaimed, "I don't know what is!" She marched up to the front of the store.

Elizabeth shook her head and followed Jessica to the counter, unable to resist a tiny smile.

Jessica pouted in the mirror, carefully outlining her lips and filling them in with crimson lipstick. She was sitting in front of Billie's vanity, putting the final touches on her makeup for the Zeta formal. This was the most important social event of the year, and she wanted to look perfect.

Tonight's going to be amazing, she thought excitedly. She had succeeded in getting Magda to invite her to the formal—and she had managed to convince Elizabeth to do a twin switch as well.

But my real coup was getting Steven and Billie out of the apartment tonight, Jessica thought with satisfaction. She had surprised them with tickets to the campus production of *Who's Afraid of Virginia Woolf?* "Just a little thank you for letting us stay here," she had told her brother and his girlfriend. Now she wouldn't have to worry about Steven and Billie messing up the scheme. They knew only the basic outline of Jessica and Elizabeth's plans for the evening. Jessica had told them they were going to the Zeta formal with blind dates supplied by Magda.

The doorbell jangled, and Jessica's heart skipped a beat. Zach had arrived. The big moment was here. She was about to make her debut into SVU society.

"Liz, will you answer that?" Jessica called, her face flushed with excitement.

142

"Hi, Zach," she heard Elizabeth say. "C'mon in. Jessica will be out in a second."

"You know, it's really uncanny," Jessica heard Zach saying in the living room. "I can't believe you're Jessica's younger sister. I would have taken you for identical twins."

Liz, don't blow it for me, Jessica silently begged her twin, rushing to finish her makeup. Elizabeth had not been pleased when she'd learned that Jessica had told Zach that Elizabeth was her younger sister visiting from high school.

Elizabeth's laughter rang through the apartment. "Uncanny, isn't it?" she agreed.

Jessica deftly swept up her hair around her head and stuck pins into it, pulling out a few wispy strands to frame her face. She quickly dabbed perfume on her neck and wrists and gave a last, satisfied look in the mirror.

She took a deep breath, then floated into the foyer, feeling regal in Elizabeth's rose-colored ball gown. She had convinced Elizabeth that they had to exchange dresses for the evening if they were going to pull off the twin switch. To compliment the elegant look of the dress, she was wearing a double-strand pearl necklace and dangly antique gold earrings with tiny tear-drop pearls at the bottom.

Zach was momentarily speechless. "You look like a princess," he breathed finally.

"And you look like my Prince Charming," Jessica replied warmly. With his muscular physique and strong features, Zach looked dashing in his black tux.

An emerald-green cummerbund brought out the green in his eyes.

Elizabeth put the back of one hand over her forehead and rolled her eyes to the ceiling, pretending as though she were about to swoon. Jessica ignored her twin's mocking gesture.

"Are you going to the Zeta dinner, too?" Zach asked, turning to Elizabeth.

"Yes, I am," Elizabeth said, quickly putting her hand by her side. "One of Jessica's friends set me up on a date."

"Well, you must be thrilled to be going to a college formal," Zach said cheerfully.

"Just thrilled," Elizabeth replied wryly.

"You can tell all your friends about it when you get back to school," Zach continued. "I bet they'll all be green with envy."

"No doubt," Elizabeth said, crossing her arms and sending Jessica a poison glance.

Jessica bit her lip nervously. If they didn't get out of the apartment soon, Zach was going to push her sister over the edge. Jessica knew that her twin, although generally calm by nature, could freak out in the most terrifying way. Elizabeth's dramatic scene at the newspaper office was a perfect example.

"I would have been so psyched to go to a college event when I was in high school," Zach went on, his tone slightly patronizing. "I always wanted to go a fraternity—"

"Uh, Zach," Jessica interrupted. "I think we should go." She pulled open the front door. "We don't want to miss a minute of the dance."

"OK, Jess," Zach agreed, picking up his jacket. "See you at the party!" he called to Elizabeth, and then he gave her a wink. "I'll try to introduce you to some of the guys in the frat." Zach smiled condescendingly. "Then you'll really have something to talk about when you get back to high school." Elizabeth looked as if she were about to burst, but she managed to give Zach a weak smile.

Jessica grabbed Zach's arm and yanked him out the door. "'Bye, Liz!" she said lightly. "See you later!"

"I'm looking forward to it," Elizabeth grumbled, slamming the door behind them.

Jessica breathed a sigh of relief as she and Zach walked out into the cool night. "I love how you look tonight," Zach whispered, wrapping his arm around her and kissing her on the cheek. "With that dress on and your hair pulled up, you look like a totally different person."

Jessica smiled modestly.

Elizabeth paced around the foyer after Jessica left, smoothing down Jessica's crushed-velvet black halter dress uncomfortably. The material was practically glued to her body, and the dress barely reached her thighs.

Elizabeth took a quick look in the mirror and stared at herself, aghast. The halter dress had a fitted bodice that flared out into a miniskirt. Her entire back and shoulders were bare, not to mention most of the rest of her body. She had never shown so much skin in her entire life.

She silently cursed herself for allowing Jessica to get her into this situation. When would she ever learn? Suddenly the doorbell rang and Elizabeth jumped.

Elizabeth took a deep breath and smoothed down her dress again. She opened the door shakily and put on her best "Jessica" smile.

Magda stood at the door between two dark, good-looking guys. She was wearing a long, slinky electric-blue silk gown that was covered in fancy beadwork. Magda looked stunning, Elizabeth thought. The dress contrasted dramatically against her fair skin and jet-black hair, and her china-blue eyes glittered like jewels. The guys were wearing black tuxedos and white cummerbunds, with red roses in their lapels. Elizabeth's mouth dropped open. This was a formal affair, and she was practically going naked.

"Hi!" Elizabeth chirped, forcing a big smile on her face. She opened the door wide, feeling as if the skin on her cheeks might crack. "Come on in."

"Jessica, this is Dan Dawson," Magda said, introducing her date.

"Nice to meet you," Elizabeth said, shaking his hand.

"And this is Frank Moretti," Magda continued. "Frank, Jessica."

"Jessica—it's a pleasure to meet you," Frank said smoothly, clasping her hand warmly. He handed her a single red rose, an enchanted look on his face. Frank looked thrilled to meet her, and Elizabeth wasn't surprised. After all, who wouldn't be pleased to see such a scantily clad date?

"Thank you," Elizabeth replied, trying to look properly enthusiastic. "That was so sweet of you." She smiled, letting the dimple in her cheek deepen— a classic Jessica Wakefield maneuver.

"Jessica, you look fabulous!" Magda enthused. "What a great dress! You're really going to bring the house down in that number."

Elizabeth groaned inwardly. That's what she was afraid of.

"Here, let me see the back," Magda ordered. Elizabeth could feel her face getting hot. She felt as if she were wearing nothing but underwear, and she was tempted to run into the bedroom and grab a sensible dress from Billie's closet. But she knew that Jessica thrived on moments like this. *Well, here goes,* Elizabeth thought, swallowing her embarrassment. She twirled dramatically for Magda and the guys, letting the dress swirl around her thighs.

"Ooh, baby!" Magda cheered. Dan and Frank whistled. Elizabeth's face flamed.

"You know," Magda began, pulling off a long silk glove, "I was thinking of going for a mini, but then I saw this dress and I just had to have it."

Elizabeth groaned. Was she going to have to talk about dresses all night? "I don't blame you," Elizabeth breathed. "It's absolutely stunning." Elizabeth fingered the tiny beaded sequins. "I love the material," she gushed. *Hmm, this isn't so hard,* she thought, beginning to get the hang of it. "And the color is simply smashing with your eyes," Elizabeth continued.

Magda beamed. "Jessica, you are just too sweet," she said.

"Well, shall we go?" Frank asked, holding out an arm for Elizabeth. Elizabeth took his arm, and they followed Magda and Dan outside.

As they got out to the car, Elizabeth pulled Magda aside to deliver the lines Jessica had made her rehearse before Zach showed up. "Magda, I think I better warn you about something before we get to the dance," she said in a low voice.

Magda looked at her with concern. "What is it?"

"You won't believe the stunt that my sister has pulled this time," Elizabeth whispered.

"Does it have something to do with the formal?" Magda asked.

Elizabeth nodded, her face grim. "Elizabeth's going to the Zeta formal, too," she said, pausing for dramatic effect. "With Zachary Marsden."

Magda's expression darkened. "How very interesting," she said.

Chapter 11

"Uh-oh," Ken said to Todd, grimacing from his perch on the ladder as Winston made his third attempt to blow up a balloon. Ken and Todd were hanging up the "Welcome to SVU" banner over the kitchen archway in Steven and Billie's apartment. The gang had made it to the campus in record time, and they were all setting up for the party. Steven and Billie had left their play at intermission so they could let them in.

"Looking good!" Todd yelled encouragingly, standing up on a wooden stool.

Puff, Puff, Winston breathed, his cheeks bulging into two pink balls as he carefully blew air into a shiny blue balloon. Ken held his breath as the skin on the balloon stretched thin. Winston's eyes bulged, and his chest heaved with the effort.

Puff, Puff, Puff . . . POP! The balloon burst in Winston's face, sending bits of rubber flying. Ken jumped and the ladder swayed dangerously.

"Whoa!" Steven said, walking by with an armful of colorful streamers. He steadied the ladder with one hand, draping a purple streamer over it with the other. "I never realized blowing up balloons could be so dangerous."

"Darnit!" Winston moaned, picking a piece of the balloon off his face and discarding it. Everybody laughed.

"Winston, you're wasting all the balloons," Enid teased from where she was setting out bowls of chips and salsa.

"Maybe we could lay them flat on the table," Winston suggested, a dejected look on his face. He picked up a big chip out of the bowl and bathed it in salsa.

"Here, Win, I'll help you," Olivia offered, joining him at the kitchen table. "I think you're trying to blow them up too big."

Winston sighed, crunching into the tortilla chip. "I guess I'm just not cut out for this balloon thing."

Ken finished fastening his side of the banner to the wall and called over to Todd, "Here you go." When Todd turned around to look, Ken tossed the hammer to him. After catching it adeptly with one hand, Todd pounded a nail into the wall and wrapped the string of the banner around it. Then he hopped down off his stool, and Ken slid to a sitting position on the ladder, watching pensively as the gang chattered together.

"Mmm, something smells good," Billie said, sniffing the air appreciatively as Lila brought out the cake and set it on the counter. "Chocolate cake! Did you bake it yourself?"

"I don't want to talk about it," Lila mumbled, reaching into a bag and setting out purple paper plates and napkins. Enid followed her to the counter, her arms laden with bottles of seltzer and soda.

Ken watched with a bemused smile as Steven crept up behind Billie. "Shh!" Steven whispered to Lila and Enid, holding a finger to his lips. Suddenly he leaped on Billie, wrapping her up in an array of pink and purple streamers.

"Steven!" Billie gasped, swatting him away. "What do you think you're doing?" She grabbed a handful of streamers from the table and looped them around his neck, drawing her to him. Soon they were giggling and kissing in a swirl of streamers.

"Hey, hey!" Todd admonished, waggling a finger at them. "Can't you two get any work done?"

Steven and Billie laughed. "Sorry," Steven said. "I guess I'm just a little excited at the thought of getting the twins out of here."

Ken rested his elbow on his thigh and propped his chin in his hand, feeling estranged from the group. The atmosphere was happy and fun, but inside Ken felt heavy. *What's this "frat thing" that Jessica and Elizabeth have been invited to?* he wondered. *How do they know frat guys in the first place?* Ken couldn't shake the uneasy feeling that Jessica was interested in another guy. A frat guy.

"Hey, Ken, you lost up there?" Todd called from the living room. "I need your help with the slides."

"I'll be with you in a sec!" Ken replied, trying to shake his suspicious thoughts. Jessica was probably just out with some of the sorority girls, he reassured himself. But what if they came back and Jessica wasn't happy to see him? Or if she had a date planned for later that night? Then a horrible thought struck him. What if Jessica came back with another guy? Ken shuddered at the thought. Not only would he be heartbroken, he would be publicly humiliated.

That's a risk I can't take, Ken decided, suddenly climbing down the ladder. It was time to take action. He wasn't going to sit around waiting for Jessica to come to him. He was going to find her.

"Were you trying to do an imitation of Rodin's *The Thinker?*" Todd asked as Ken walked into the living room. Todd was sitting on the floor, a collection of slides spread out in front of him. Enid and Lila were setting out food on the coffee table.

Lila dropped a handful of forks with a loud clatter. "Todd," she asked, "did you just make a cultural reference?"

Enid giggled and Todd scowled. "Very funny, Lila," he said.

"Actually, I was being *The Thinker,*" Ken said. "And I've come up with an amazing idea." He pulled Todd into the privacy of the hall.

"I wonder what they're up to," Ken heard Lila say to Enid.

Ken looked around carefully and spoke in a low voice. "Instead of waiting for the twins to come back, why don't we surprise them at the fraternity?" he suggested. "How could they want to stay with their boyfriends around?"

Todd's eyes lit up. Ken knew he was aching to see Elizabeth. "That's a great idea!" Todd said enthusiastically. But a moment later his expression changed. "But what about the plan?" he asked worriedly. "We don't want to undermine all our efforts."

"This way they'll get a double surprise," Ken reasoned. "First their boyfriends at the fraternity, then all their friends at the apartment."

Todd grinned. "I'm in, man. I can't wait to see the look on Liz's face!"

"Mmm, you smell nice," Frank said, burying his head in Elizabeth's neck as they danced at the Zeta formal.

Elizabeth grimaced. "Thank you," she said tightly.

Frank wasn't the only man paying attention to Elizabeth. Just about every male head had turned as Elizabeth had walked across the dance floor, the velvet of her dress clinging to every curve of her body. *Now I know what it feels like to be Jessica,* Elizabeth thought. And she didn't like the feeling.

Frank whirled Elizabeth around, and her skirt flew into the air, revealing her upper thighs. Elizabeth frantically smoothed her skirt down, her face flaming. She could not believe she was out in public in this attire. It was so humiliating.

Elizabeth was not only embarrassed, she was furious. She and Magda had chatted together by the hors d'oeuvres table after they had first arrived. The more

Magda had talked, the more outraged Elizabeth had become. Elizabeth could not believe the horrible things that Jessica had said about her. Jessica had not only told Magda the party last Saturday night was her idea, but she had said Elizabeth wanted to have an all-guy party because she was man crazy. She, Elizabeth! Man crazy!

"You have such beautiful hair," Frank murmured, running a hand through the long silky hair cascading down Elizabeth's back.

"Thank you," Elizabeth replied curtly, ticking off the insults in her mind: conniving, selfish, manipulative, a flirt. *A flirt!* She clenched at Frank's back with her nails, her fury building.

"Oh, Jessica," Frank moaned, misinterpreting the signal. He pulled her closer and wrapped his arms around her. Elizabeth backed away, resisting a shudder of disgust. Frank was actually a nice guy, but Elizabeth had no desire to be in his arms. *I'd give anything for Todd to suddenly materialize here,* she thought. Preferably with a long coat for her to wear.

The music changed to a popular rock beat, and Elizabeth breathed a sigh of relief. She dropped her arms from Frank's shoulders and swayed along with the music.

"You know, Dan is really infatuated with Magda," Frank said.

"Mmm," Elizabeth said. *A schemer.* Jessica had said her sister was a schemer and that she always had to cover for her. *What a laugh*, thought Elizabeth. She was the one always covering for Jessica. Jessica had actually drawn a perfect portrait of herself and called it Elizabeth.

"Magda is all Dan ever talks about," Frank went on. "Magda this, Magda that."

"Is that so?" Elizabeth replied, replaying her conversation with Magda in her head. "You really are noble to put up with a sister like Elizabeth," Magda had said. "But then, I guess one doesn't really have a choice when it comes to sisters."

"I guess not," Elizabeth had agreed.

"I really think Dan would be great for Magda," Frank continued. "He's athletic, nice, and he comes from old money."

"Mmm, I'll put in a good word for him," Elizabeth offered half-heartedly. To think that Jessica had cajoled her into doing this twin switch on the grounds that she had been covering for Elizabeth at the Thetas. *Covering for me!* Elizabeth fumed. Jessica had basically shot any chance Elizabeth would ever have of getting into the Thetas. She felt like marching up to Jessica right now and blowing her cover. Not that she really cared about the Thetas. It was just the principle of the thing.

"If only Magda would give Dan half a chance, they'd be a great couple," Frank went on.

Elizabeth stifled a yawn. Nothing could interest her less than college couples or sororities.

"Why are girls so messed up, Jessica?" Frank wondered aloud. Elizabeth shook her head. If he only knew!

∘   ∘   ∘

"Jessica, I had no idea you were such a great dancer," Zach said, lifting her high in the air and spinning her around.

"Are you trying to sweep me off my feet?" Jessica asked, laughing breathlessly as he returned her to the ground.

Zach grinned. "I want everybody to see what a fabulous date I've got for the formal."

Jessica smiled with pleasure. Everybody could definitely see them. They were in the center of the dance floor, and they were getting lots of attention.

Jessica was amazed at her own brilliance. This was an all-time feat. Here she was flaunting her date with Zach in front of everybody and totally getting away with it. She couldn't wait to tell Ken all about it. But then she remembered—Ken would not be thrilled to hear about this scheme.

Zach pulled her in close to him. "But I want you all for myself," he said softly, rubbing his cheek against her. They swayed gently to the music.

Jessica rested her head on Zach's shoulder, her gaze wandering over the crowded dance floor. She caught sight of Elizabeth in Frank's arms in the corner. Elizabeth looked like a wooden doll, holding herself stiffly as her date laughed. Jessica tried to get her attention, but she felt another pair of eyes boring into her. It was Magda. She was in the arms of some boring-looking guy with dark hair, and she was sending Jessica a look of pure venom.

Jessica averted her eyes quickly, stifling a sigh. She realized that she was actually searching for Ken.

She shook her head and focused on Zach. He was telling some story about a formal party at his frat at Dartmouth.

"Soon everybody was in jeans, slam dancing on the floor to industrial music," Zach said. "Until the police showed up with a noise complaint and kicked everybody out." Zach laughed, remembering. "'You call this screeching and clanging *music*?' the cops said. I think they were more upset by our choice of tunes than by the noise we were making."

Jessica forced a laugh. "Oh, that's so funny," she said.

Suddenly Zach's expression turned serious. He lifted Jessica's chin up and looked her in the eyes. "Jessica," he began softly, "I've had the most wonderful time with you this week."

"Me, too," Jessica whispered, wondering why the words felt empty.

"I loved our picnic on the quad the other day," Zach said. "Even if you did make a rather quick exit."

Jessica laughed, but her mind flashed to the romantic picnic Ken had made for her on their second date. It was on a deserted strand of beach up the coast. Ken had packed a gourmet meal and brought along a beat-up old tape deck. They had lain together on a blanket in the sand, talking for hours by the light of two twinkling lanterns. And then Ken had kissed her, a sandy, salty kiss that seemed to go on forever.

"You never did explain why you had to leave so fast," Zach said, a questioning look in his eyes.

"Now, Zach, you don't want to spoil all the mystery, do you?" Jessica said, laughing flirtatiously. "I thought mystery is what keeps a romance going."

"Well, it's certainly working," Zach said in a throaty voice. He looked her in the eyes and leaned in to kiss her. Jessica closed her eyes and forced herself to relax in Zach's embrace, trying to lose herself in the kiss. But all she could think of was the goodbye kiss Ken had given her the week before. It had been so sweet and tender. "Be good," Ken had said, touching her cheek lightly.

Jessica wrenched herself away from Zach, feeling a wave of longing for Ken.

Zach looked her in the eyes, his piercing green eyes intense. "Tonight with you is perfect," he whispered.

Jessica didn't answer and leaned her head on his chest. Everything would be perfect, she thought, if only she could concentrate on the college guy she was with instead of the high school boy she had left at home.

"Jessica!" Magda hissed to Elizabeth, steering Dan toward her on the dance floor. Elizabeth looked up, a feeling of dread seeping into her pores. She didn't think she could handle having her character slandered any further. And she was in no mood to talk about sororities or dresses.

"You won't believe this," Magda said, whispering over Dan's shoulder. "Your conniving twin sister Elizabeth has actually done me a favor. Alison Quinn just told me that Zach is really only a—" she mouthed the words—"junior in high school."

"What?" Elizabeth exclaimed. "But I thought he's taking classes here."

Magda held a red-tipped finger up to her lips. "He's just taking a couple of advanced placement classes at SVU," she explained in a whisper. "His older brother is in Zeta, and the guys thought it would be funny to pass off Zach as a junior transfer student."

Elizabeth mouth dropped open. This was the most interesting thing anybody had said to her all evening. All this time Jessica had been trying to manipulate Zach, and he had been doing the same thing to her. Jessica had been so worried that Zach would find out she was in high school, and he was in high school himself. Elizabeth stifled a laugh, feeling vindicated. It looked like the great schemer had been out-schemed for once.

"Can you imagine how humiliated I would have been if I started dating a high school boy?" Magda continued.

Elizabeth shook her head, forcing a somber expression on her face. "It's absolutely unthinkable," she said seriously.

"Tell your sister the joke's on her," Magda crowed. Then she paused. "Scratch that. I'll tell her myself."

Elizabeth smiled as Magda and Dan danced away, feeling her anger melt away. After all of Jessica's plotting and scheming, she was finally going to get a taste of her own medicine. She couldn't wait to see the look on her sister's face.

Chapter 12

"That's it!" Ken exclaimed, pointing to an ivy-covered red brick building with a big *Zeta* banner hanging on it. "JUST PARTY" was spray painted in bold white block letters across the front of the building.

Todd shut off the headlights and swung the car into reverse, smoothly backing down Cherry Lane and around the corner into a side street. "Let's go," Todd said, cutting the engine and jumping out.

Ken stepped onto the crunchy gravel, a sick feeling in the pit of his stomach. He was about to find out what Jessica had been up to all week, and he wasn't sure he was ready to face it.

Ken and Todd had gotten directions to the Zeta house from Billie, and she had been distinctly uneasy. "It'll put a wrench in the plan," Billie had argued. "Why don't you just wait until they get home?" But Ken had insisted, and Billie had reluctantly agreed. "OK," she had sighed. "It's on Greek Row—Cherry

161

Lane." Now Ken was really concerned. *Was Billie really only worried about the plan?* he wondered. *Or was she worried about something else as well?*

"Maybe we can just blend in with the crowd until we find them," Todd said as they crept across the yard to the Theta house. Hugging the walls of the building, they made their way silently to the front door. A majestic black wooden door with a big brass knocker stared at them imposingly.

Todd turned the latch carefully, opened the door a crack, and peeked through. "Whew, quite a spread," he whistled softly.

Ken peered in as well, sucking in his breath as he took in the atmosphere. He felt like he'd been transported back in time to an eighteenth century French ball. The vast hall had marble floors and high ceilings, and a sparkling crystal chandelier illuminated the dance floor. White tablecloths and tall glass candlesticks adorned the tables. An elaborate buffet was set up, and a live band was playing up on a stage. There was a mean-looking bouncer in a suit at the door taking tickets.

Suddenly the bouncer turned in their direction. "Todd!" Ken hissed, slipping out of the doorway. Todd quickly let go of the door and the boys fled across the lawn.

"Now what?" Ken asked, after they had ducked around the side of the building, panting rapidly. "There's no way that guy's going to let us in. We're not dressed in formal attire, and we're not college guys."

"And we're not Zetas, and we haven't been invited," Todd added.

Ken leaned against the ivy-covered wall, trying to catch his breath. "Looks like we only have one choice at this point," he said. "We're going to have to sneak in."

Todd nodded. "We really just need a few minutes. All we have to do is get in, surprise the twins, and get out."

Ken thought for a moment. "There must be a side entrance somewhere."

Todd scanned the side of the building. "I don't see any kind of door," he said. Then his eyes lit up. "But I do see a another kind of entrance," he amended, pointing to a large French window about ten feet up the wall. Todd grabbed onto an ivy vine and shimmied up the wall, supporting himself with his good foot.

"I'm spotting you, buddy," Ken said, grabbing onto the ivy and following close behind.

When he reached the window, Todd wedged his foot into the crack of a brick and held onto a ledge for support. After finding his own foothold, Ken joined him and peered into the window. From their vantage point, they had a clear view of the dance floor.

Ken's heart pounded in his chest as he scanned the crowded dance floor, looking for Jessica. His gaze fell on a couple making out passionately in the center of the dance floor. The woman was about 5'6" and had long blond hair. Ken held his breath, waiting for them to turn around. The woman's face slowly came into view. She had a rounded chin and she wore glasses. Ken exhaled sharply. It wasn't Jessica. *Where was she?* he wondered.

Then he caught sight of her, and relief coursed through his veins. Jessica was standing by the buffet table, looking incredibly sexy as usual in a black velvet dress. She was talking to some science nerd, and she looked completely miserable.

"Todd, there's Jessica!" Ken said excitedly, nudging him. Todd didn't answer. "Todd?" Ken asked. "What's wrong?" He looked over at his friend. Todd was staring at the dance floor, a look of pure astonishment on his face. Ken followed his gaze.

Elizabeth was smack in the center of the dance floor, looking breathtaking in a rose-colored gown. She was whirling around in the arms of some guy, a jock. And she was laughing up at him flirtatiously, a look of pure adoration on her face.

Todd's face was ashen. "I can't believe this," he said. "No wonder Elizabeth wanted to stay at college." Todd's voice crackled with bitterness. "She really wanted to stay in that guy's arms."

Ken was speechless. "What a fool I've been," Todd muttered in disgust. Holding onto the window ledge with one arm, he kicked violently at the wall of the Theta house with his cast, causing pieces of red brick to fall to the ground. Todd grabbed hold of the ivy and slid recklessly down the building, landing on his good foot and crouching to absorb the shock. Ken followed quickly behind, hurrying after Todd.

"It was all a lie," Todd muttered, limping rapidly to the car. "The internship, the professor—all a lie."

"Todd, where are you going?" Ken asked.

"I'm getting out of here," Todd said, his voice

hoarse with hurt and anger. "I'm going back to Sweet Valley. If Elizabeth wants some Big Man on Campus, she can have him."

Ken barred his way, folding his arms across his chest. "Doesn't Elizabeth mean anything to you?" he asked.

"What?" Todd asked, his eyes flashing with anger. "What are you talking about? Of course she does."

"Then why are you going to let her go so easily?" Ken pressed, a challenge in his eyes. "I didn't realize you were the type to just give up without a fight."

Todd thought for a minute, then his face filled with determination. "You're right," he said. "Let's go in there, and find out the truth for once and for all."

"That's my man," Ken said. But then they stopped and looked at each other. How were they going to get in?

"Looks like there's only way to ruin a party," Todd said, a wounded smile playing on his lips.

"Crash it," Ken agreed.

"Yeah, pledge week was just the worst," Frank admitted, shaking his head. He speared a piece of mustard chicken with his cocktail fork and stuffed it into his mouth, chuckling to himself.

Elizabeth sighed and bit into a stuffed mushroom. She was standing with Frank by the buffet table, a plate of hors d'oeuvres in her hand. Frank had been babbling on for the last half hour about his experiences as a Zeta pledge. Elizabeth couldn't remember ever feeling so bored.

"Did I tell you about the time they made us dress

165

up as pirates and walk the plank?" Frank asked, his eyes lighting up with the memory.

No, but I'm sure you're going to, Elizabeth thought. She smiled up at Frank. "I don't think I've heard about that yet."

"Oh, wait till you hear this one," Frank said, his face becoming animated. "The brothers drove us out to the quarry and blindfolded us. We had to walk along this long wooden plank in the rain until we reached the end. And then they yelled, "Walk the plank, pledge!" And we had to jump out into nothingness." Frank shivered at the memory of it. "Can you imagine?" he asked Elizabeth.

"No, I really can't," Elizabeth replied.

"It's an unbelievable feeling," Frank went on. "You just leap out into the air, and you don't know where you're going to land." Frank laughed softly to himself. "Oh, yeah, that was a great one."

"Sounds like it," Elizabeth said, taking a sip of sparkling apple cider from a champagne flute. That was the stupidest thing she'd ever heard.

"Yeah, it really is a rite of passage," Frank added. "They have something similar in sororities, too . . ."

Elizabeth tuned him out, gritting her teeth in frustration. If she heard one more word about fraternities or sororities, she was going to scream.

Suddenly her attention was caught by some commotion at the door.

"Hey, what's going on?" Frank asked, looking over at the front door.

Elizabeth squinted through the crowd. It looked

like two big guys in jeans and T-shirts were trying to crash the party. One of them had a cast on his leg. Elizabeth blinked and looked again. *Todd?*

Elizabeth's heart raced. "Excuse me," she said to Frank, dropping her plate on the table and running over to the door.

"Todd!" she called, throwing herself into his arms. Both Todd and Ken looked totally shocked.

"Jessica?" Todd said, recoiling a step. Elizabeth just shook her head silently and gave him a passionate kiss.

"Hey, that's my date!" Frank yelled, running up to the doorway.

"She's not your date, she's my girlfriend!" Todd shouted angrily.

Frank looked surprised. "Your girlfriend?" he asked. Then he pushed Todd out of the way. "Well, she's mine tonight."

Todd shoved Frank back harder. "She's not yours tonight or any night!"

Elizabeth was about to protest that she wasn't *anybody's any night* when three of Frank's frat brothers materialized.

"Well, what do we have here?" a hulking guy in a suit said, inspecting Todd like he was an insect under a jar.

"Looks like some high school jerk wants a piece of the action," the second guy put in.

"We'll give him some action," the third guy threatened, opening the door wide. Elizabeth bit her lip as they picked up Todd unceremoniously and threw him out onto the front lawn.

"Oh, Jessica," Zach murmured, burying his head in her hair as they swayed gently to the soft music. "I wish this night would go on forever."

I wish this night would end, Jessica thought. Then she reprimanded herself. After all the trouble she'd gone to to get to this event, she should be enjoying herself. Jessica wrapped her arms around Zach's waist and rested her head on his shoulder. She closed her eyes, letting the music caress her body and trying to lose herself in it.

Suddenly she felt a firm tap on her shoulder. Jessica looked up and gasped. Ken was standing right in front of her, wearing jeans and a T-shirt. Jessica's heart leapt, and then began pounding. "Ken!" she exclaimed, quickly dropping her arms from Zach's waist. "What are you doing here?"

"I was hoping to surprise you," Ken said, his face a mixture of anger and hurt. "But I guess I'm the one who got the surprise."

"Ken, you don't understand," Jessica said, desperately searching for an excuse. "This isn't what it looks like." She began babbling nonsensically. "Magda set me up on a blind date. For the Zeta formal. The Zeta formal is *the* social event of the year, and Magda said I absolutely *had* to come to this affair if I wanted to get into the Thetas."

Ken looked uncertain. "And you know how important the Thetas are to me," Jessica finished, staring at him imploringly.

Ken weighed her words. "It doesn't look like a

blind date from the way you were dancing," he said.

Zach was looking back and forth from Jessica to Ken, trying to make sense of the situation. "A blind date!" he burst out angrily. "If you call this a blind date—"

But Ken cut him off. "No wonder you wanted to stay at SVU!" he said to Jessica, his tone bitter and accusatory. "You didn't want a college life. You wanted a college *man*."

"Ken, I can explain!" Jessica said, grabbing his arm.

But Ken shook her off her hand in disgust. "I don't want to hear any more of your excuses, Jessica," he said flatly. "A relationship without trust is no relationship at all." He turned away and stomped off.

Jessica looked after him as he strode angrily through the sea of dancers, pain stabbing at her heart. Suddenly she knew she was still in love with Ken—even if he was in high school. Who would have guessed?

Chapter 13

"Hey, what's all the commotion about?" a muscular guy asked, making his way to the bouncer at the door.

"What's the deal with those guys?" a tall, willowy woman dressed in all black wanted to know.

"I think it has something to do with those blond twins," a woman explained to her friend.

"Who are they, anyway?" her friend wondered.

Elizabeth's face burned as she stood by the doorway, unsure which way to turn. The twins had created quite a scene. A crowd had gathered around Elizabeth, and dozens of people were staring.

Suddenly an angry guy elbowed his way violently through the crowd.

"Ken!" Elizabeth cried, reaching out a hand to stop him. But he stormed past her and slammed out the front door. The crowd buzzed noisily.

Elizabeth hesitated, looking from the front door to the dance floor. She was tempted to run after Ken and Todd, but she didn't want to leave Jessica alone. Elizabeth made up her mind quickly. She would find Jessica and insist they go after their boyfriends together. And if Jessica wouldn't leave, then Elizabeth would go alone. She was finished with this affair.

"Excuse me," she said to the people around her, squeezing her way through the crowd and weaving her way across the packed dance floor. She caught sight of Jessica in the middle of the dance floor with Zach and hurried up to them.

But then she stopped. It looked like Magda had gotten to Jessica first. *Well, this is one conversation I want to hear*, Elizabeth thought.

A small smile flickered across Elizabeth's face as she approached. It sounded like Jessica had turned on her "excuse voice" full force.

"Listen, Magda," Jessica said. "I'm really sorry about the disturbance. I don't know what happened. We had absolutely no idea these guys were coming. In fact, we barely know them."

But Magda cut her off with a wave of an elegant hand. "Elizabeth," she said. "I don't know exactly what's going on, but I want to thank you."

Jessica's mouth dropped open. "Thank me?" she asked.

"Yes, thank you," Magda replied, grinning evilly. "If you hadn't been here with Zach tonight, I probably could have been arrested for robbing the cradle."

"Robbing the cradle?" Jessica echoed, looking thoroughly confused.

"A mature women should never go out with an

adolescent boy," Magda explained. "It's terrible for her reputation."

Jessica's brow furrowed and she looked at Zach suspiciously. Suddenly, she seemed to understand.

Bingo! Elizabeth thought.

"You mean—?" Jessica began.

"Exactly," Magda said. "This supposed college man is actually a high school boy. In fact he's a junior." Magda smiled sweetly and let the final bomb drop before turning away. "Just like you," she added. Elizabeth tried not to laugh as Jessica and Zach stared at each other, dumbfounded.

"Well, I guess I'll get back to my date," Magda said pleasantly, smiling at the two of them. "Enjoy your evening!" Magda walked a few steps and then stopped, turning back. "Oh, by the way," she said to the twins, "you're welcome at the Theta house any time—both of you."

Jessica stared at Magda in silence, trembling as if she were shell-shocked.

"Oh, and Jessica," Magda said, turning toward Elizabeth, "you really should try to get along with your sister. Family is so important."

"Thanks, Magda," Elizabeth said, trying to contain her laughter. "I'll try." Elizabeth hooked her arm through Magda's. "Why don't we go find our dates?" she asked, her eyes glittering mischievously. "It looks like these two have a lot to talk about."

"You lied!" Jessica screamed, wheeling on Zach as soon as Magda and Elizabeth were out of earshot.

She stared at Zach with her arms folded over her chest, waiting for an explanation. Suddenly he really looked like a high school boy. Now she understood why he hadn't seemed so smooth. And why he was so easy to fool. She was mortified. How dare he humiliate her in front of all the Thetas?

"I lied? You lied!" Zach screamed back.

"I only lied because I had to," Jessica defended herself hotly. "You're the one who assumed I was in college."

"Obviously I thought you were in college," Zach scoffed. "You were having a college party. That is no excuse!"

"Well, do you have a better one?" Jessica asked, tapping her foot on the ground.

"My older brother is in Zeta and the guys thought it would be funny to pass me off as a college junior," Zach said, looking abashed. He glanced down at the ground. "I guess it's not very funny, is it?"

"Not very," Jessica said. She was seething. All this time she had been so thrilled to be dating a college man, and he was only a high school boy after all. She couldn't believe Zach had the nerve to lie to her like that. And the most mortifying part was that she had bought the whole thing.

"Well, what's your story?" Zach demanded, looking as angry as she felt.

"Elizabeth and I are visiting my brother Steven," Jessica explained, embarrassed. "We wanted to get a feel for college life."

"So Elizabeth isn't your little sister in high school, she's—"

"My identical twin," Jessica admitted.

Zach hit himself in the side of the face. "How could I have been so stupid?"

"It is kind of amazing," Jessica agreed.

"You're one to talk!" Zach said hotly. "You're the one who believed that I had transferred from Dartmouth."

"Well, of course I did," Jessica replied. "I would have never dreamed you would have been making it up. Especially after all those stories about the kids in Virginia and your father and the CIA." Jessica could feel herself getting worked up as she thought about it. All that talk about honesty. And Jessica had felt so guilty. She felt like kicking herself. How could she have been so naive?

"Well, that part's true," Zach said quickly.

"And that toast in the restaurant to honesty," Jessica said, getting madder and madder. "Zach, you're such a hypocrite."

Zach looked at her in amazement. "Me? What about you?"

They both stared at each other with their arms folded across their chests, identical expressions of self-righteousness on their faces. Suddenly, Jessica couldn't help herself—she cracked a smile. And then they both started laughing hysterically.

"We're both hypocrites," Jessica managed to blurt out through her laughter, holding on to her sides.

"No wonder you had no idea what the East Coast was like," Zach said, still laughing. "Have you ever been to the shore?" he asked.

Jessica shook her head.

"Atlantic City?" Zach asked.

Jessica shook her head again.

Zach lifted his champagne flute, imitating the toast he had made in the restaurant. "Well, Jessica," Zach said, his face somber. "Here's to honesty!"

"To honesty," Jessica echoed, trying to keep a straight face. They clinked glasses and burst out laughing. Soon they were laughing so hard they were crying. Couples dancing near them began to look at them strangely.

"Zach, we better get off the dance floor. Some of your fraternity brothers might see us," Jessica said, unable to contain her laughter.

"Or some of your sorority sisters," Zach added.

As they wiped away tears of laughter, Jessica remembered something—Ken.

"Excuse me, I have to find my boyfriend," Jessica explained.

Zach nodded. "Listen, Jessica," he said, taking her hand in his. "I really have enjoyed getting to know you."

"Me too," Jessica said softly. "And that's the truth!" she added, grinning broadly.

"Well, maybe we'll meet again," Zach said. "Under more honest circumstances."

"I'll see you in two years!" Jessica called to him, waving as she walked away to find Elizabeth. "In English 101!"

"Liz, do you see Todd's or Ken's car anywhere over there?" Jessica yelled from the far side of the Zeta house.

"No, there's no sign of them," Elizabeth shouted back.

Jessica sighed. They had been hunting around for Todd and Ken for the last fifteen minutes, but their two boyfriends were nowhere to be found. Jessica felt totally depressed. Just when she had realized how much Ken meant to her, she had lost him for good. *If only he hadn't shown up at the party*, she thought in frustration. Then she would have ended things with Zach and everything would have been fine with Ken.

"Where do you think they went?" Elizabeth asked, joining her twin in the street.

"They're probably already on the highway home," Jessica said morosely.

"I guess we should head back to Steven and Billie's," Elizabeth decided, shivering as a gust of cool air hit her body.

Jessica kicked at a pebble in the road. "Well, we really messed things up this time," she said. "Didn't we, Liz?"

"We!" Elizabeth exclaimed hotly.

"OK, OK, *I* did," Jessica amended. "But now we're in this together."

Elizabeth's expression was gloomy. "You're right, unfortunately." She shook her head. "I don't know how you manage to get me involved in these things."

But Jessica wasn't paying attention—her mind was focused on Ken. There had to be some way to fix things up with him. "Maybe I can tell him that it was all just an act, that Zach liked me and I didn't like him," she thought out loud. "And that I didn't want to hurt his feelings."

Elizabeth whirled around, looking at her sister in shock. "Jessica Wakefield, don't you ever learn?"

"Learn what?" Jessica asked.

"To tell the truth!" Elizabeth replied.

"The truth?" Jessica asked, looking at Elizabeth with disdain. "Liz, you've got to be kidding. You want me to call Ken up and say, "Oh, sorry, I was cheating on you for a week, but now I'd like to have a long-distance relationship?"

"Exactly," Elizabeth said.

"You sound just like Billie," Jessica pointed out. "She told me to come clean to everybody last week." Jessica shook her head. "I don't think either of you live in the real world."

"Haven't you ever heard the expression *The truth will set you free*?" Elizabeth asked.

"Yeah, free from a relationship," Jessica scoffed.

"Jessica, just where did it get you to lie to Zach all week?" Elizabeth demanded.

"Well, it would have been fine if Zach hadn't turned out to be a total fraud," Jessica replied.

"No, Jessica, it would have been a disaster. At some point, the truth about your age would have come out."

Jessica shrugged her shoulders. "So I would have dealt with it then."

"Jess," Elizabeth explained, "don't you see that you make your life totally complicated?"

"That's why my life is so interesting," Jessica said

with a smile. "Not like yours and Mr. Boring Todd Wilkins."

Elizabeth threw her hands up in the air. "Fine, I give up."

"So what are we going to tell Todd and Ken?" Jessica asked. "Maybe we should say we were set up." She played with the idea in her mind for a moment. Suddenly she narrowed her eyes. "I've got it!" she exclaimed, snapping her fingers. "We'll say we had to go with blind dates to the Zeta formal as a Theta rush gag. And that we had to pretend we liked it. That's it! It's perfect!" Her eyes were shining. "Liz, what do you think?"

"Jessica, I know exactly what I'm telling Todd," Elizabeth said firmly. "The truth."

Jessica turned worried eyes to her sister. "The whole truth?"

"And nothing but the truth," Elizabeth pledged.

Jessica bit her lip. "Liz, you can't do that to me," she said nervously. "If you tell Todd, then he'll tell Ken everything, and—"

Elizabeth cut her off. "Jessica, begging me isn't going to work this time. I cannot believe you have the gall to ask me to do anything for you after all the horrible things you said to Magda about me."

"C'mon, Lizzie. I had no choice. You know I was desperate," Jessica explained. "And you don't care about the Thetas anyway."

"That is not the point," Elizabeth said. "The point is that you pretended you were doing me a favor. You cajoled me into going to this party on the grounds that I needed to get in good with the Thetas." Elizabeth's expression grew more and more outraged as she spoke. "Just because I don't want to be a member of a stupid sorority doesn't mean I want my reputation completely smeared before I even start college."

"Take it easy, Liz," Jessica said. "It all worked out in the end, anyway. Your reputation hasn't been affected at all, and we're both still in good with the sorority. Magda said we could come by anytime."

"You've pushed me too far this time, Jessica Wakefield," Elizabeth said sternly. "I did you a huge favor tonight, and my relationship might be ruined because of it. I refuse to make any further sacrifices for your insane schemes."

"But, Liz, you've got to stick by me," Jessica wailed. "We're twins."

"The subject is closed," Elizabeth replied.

Jessica opened her mouth and shut it. There was no point in arguing any further. Elizabeth had the "I mean business" tone in her voice that Jessica particularly loathed.

"So it looks like you don't have any choice but to tell the truth, huh?" Elizabeth said as they approached Steven and Billie's apartment complex.

"Hmmph," Jessica pouted, stamping her foot in frustration. Elizabeth really had her over a barrel. "The truth," she said with a groan. It was really against her principles to come clean. *The truth*, she repeated to herself. *What a nightmare*.

Chapter 14

Elizabeth opened the front door of Steven and Billie's apartment and gasped.

"Surprise!" everybody yelled, throwing multicolored dots of confetti in the air. Elizabeth looked around the apartment in a state of shock. All of their friends were there—Olivia, Enid, and Penny. Winston and Maria. Amy, Jean, and Sandy. Annie Whitman and Cheryl Thomas. Even Bruce Patman! Steven and Billie's cozy little apartment had been transformed. Streamers and brightly colored balloons adorned the walls, a big banner proclaiming "Welcome to SVU!" hung over the kitchen archway, and a huge photo collage of the twins stood propped up on the mantle.

"Congratulations, Liz!" Olivia said, rushing up to Jessica and throwing her arms around her. "I hereby dub you 'Queen of SVU.'" She ceremoniously placed a fuchsia party hat with "Queen Elizabeth" written on it on Jessica's head.

Elizabeth's mouth dropped open as Olivia mistook Jessica for herself. What was going on? Their friends never confused them. Then she looked down at her outfit and realized that she and Jessica were still dressed in each other's personalities. She glanced over at Jessica with a smile. Jessica gave her a wink.

"Way to go, Jess," Amy said, giving Elizabeth a big hug. "For the latest member of the Thetas," she added, putting a black "Sister Jessica" nun's cap on her head.

Jessica and Elizabeth took off the hats and switched them, shaking their heads and pointing at each other.

"What—?" Amy began.

Elizabeth shook her head. "Don't ask."

"Looks like the terrible twins are up to something," Bruce said with a grin.

"You guys are going to turn this campus upside down," Annie Whitman said with a smile, shaking her head.

"Well, I think it's an awesome idea for you two to stay at SVU," Winston put in, coming up to the twins. "Care for a whiff?" he asked, bending down to show his flower.

"Winston!" Jessica and Elizabeth moaned in unison. Everybody laughed.

Elizabeth laughed too, but she felt a bit unsettled. She was thrilled to see all their friends, but a little surprised that they weren't more upset. *Well, maybe they're just trying to be good sports*, Elizabeth reasoned. *Maybe they don't want to show us how they really feel*. She looked around for Todd and Ken, but they were nowhere to be seen.

"OK, OK, everybody into the living room," Billie ordered, clapping her hands. Bits of pink and purple streamers were caught in her silky chestnut hair.

"The festivities are about to begin!" Steven announced, looking ridiculous with a king's crown on his head.

Steven and Billie ushered the twins into the living room.

"Here you are!" Billie said, patting a place on the sofa for the twins. "Best seats in the house." Elizabeth looked at Jessica questioningly as all their friends gathered around them, taking seats on the rug.

Billie stood in front of the group and cleared her throat. "I would like to welcome you all to the premier screening of "This is Your Life at Sweet Valley High," brought to you direct from the Sweet Valley gang and dedicated to Jessica and Elizabeth."

Wild clapping and cheering greeted Billie's introduction.

Elizabeth blinked, feeling tears come to her eyes. She had almost forgotten how wonderful it was to be surrounded by all her friends. And they had gone to so much trouble.

"Contributions will be accepted after the show," Steven added.

"Steven!" Billie protested, whacking him in the stomach.

Steven dimmed the lights and flicked on the slide projector, aiming the nose toward the opposite wall. A larger-than-life image appeared on the wall. It was the Sweet Valley High cheerleaders in a pyramid with Jessica and Amy on top, holding their arms up in the air.

"The Sweet Valley cheerleaders at the final game of the season," Amy narrated.

"Nice job!" Winston said.

"Just wait," Amy said, clicking the projector. The next slide showed the pyramid falling, as all the girls collapsed in a tangle of arms and legs. Amy and Jessica burst out laughing.

"Oh gosh," Amy gasped. "Remember how we staged that at the Big Mesa game?"

"Just to humiliate Heather," Jessica chimed in, wiping tears out of her eyes.

But Elizabeth noticed that Jessica's face got serious fast. Was she feeling nostalgic for cheerleading?

"Olivia?" Amy prompted, handing Olivia the remote.

"The special Fall sports edition of *The Oracle*," Olivia announced, clicking to a slide showing Olivia and Elizabeth proudly holding up a pasted-up blueprint.

"Hey, is that me?" Bruce asked, leaning forward to take a closer look at the tennis shot. Bruce was a star player on the tennis team.

"Of course not, Bruce," Jessica said. "Those are only photos of the winners."

"Jessica, if this weren't your party, I would clobber you," Bruce growled.

Elizabeth smiled as she waited for the next slide, which showed a shocked Elizabeth as all the photographs cascaded to the floor. "Oops!" Olivia said. "Avalanche!"

"Oh, Olivia, remember how mad Penny was?" Elizabeth asked.

"I thought she was going to explode," Olivia giggled, handing the remote to Lila. "All her hard work—ruined!"

Elizabeth felt a pang of longing for *The Oracle*. *The Oracle* staff almost felt like family to her. And at the school paper, she was given both respect and responsibility. Unlike the *Chronicle*, where she had just been a pawn for Petherbrook's abuse.

"Ladies and gentlemen," Lila said, clicking the slide projector, "the famous Wakefield Jeep!" The slide showed the whole gang squeezed into Jessica and Elizabeth's new Jeep Wrangler, waving wildly.

"What a set of wheels!" Winston said in admiration.

"How did we all fit in there?" Jessica wondered.

"And now for the romantic part of the evening's entertainment," Enid said, taking over. She clicked rapidly through a series of romantic shots—Elizabeth and Todd walking alone on the beach, hand in hand; Ken and Jessica kneeling together in the sand, building a sandcastle; Elizabeth and Todd laughing together in the center of a group at the Dairi Burger; Ken holding Jessica up in the air on the football field; and finally close-ups of both couples kissing. The effect was like a romantic montage sequence in a film.

Whistles and catcalls followed the shots.

"Hubba hubba!" Winston shouted.

"Looking hot!" Bruce added.

"Hey, guys, keep it clean. This is a family show,"

Steven said with a grin, taking the remote from Enid. "Last, but not least, I present the Wakefield family." Steven clicked through a series of shots of the Wakefields skiing in Colorado during a family vacation—Mr. and Mrs. Wakefield standing on skis at the top of a snow-covered mountain, Billie and Steven laughing as they pummeled each other with snowballs; Elizabeth speeding down a snowy white trail, ski poles tucked neatly behind her, Jessica tumbling down the mountain after her, skis flying, and finally, the whole family together in front of the ski lodge, smiling into the camera with their arms slung around each other's waists.

Tears were streaming down Elizabeth's face. She was leaving all of this behind. Sweet Valley, *The Oracle*, her friends and family. And Todd. Pain stabbed Elizabeth's heart. Todd had driven all the way to SVU to surprise her, only to find her out on a date with a frat guy. Where was he now? Was he back in Sweet Valley already? Had she ruined things with him forever?

Elizabeth glanced over at Jessica. She was curled up on the couch, and it looked like her eyes were misting as well.

"Well, that's it!" Billie said cheerfully, clicking the slide projector off briskly and flipping on the lights. Elizabeth blinked and fumbled in her bag for a Kleenex.

"Time for the second part of the show," Winston announced. "Food fest!"

Lila sat down in front of the coffee table and

began slicing thick pieces of chocolate cake. Annie added scoops of ice cream to the plates, and Enid poured sparkling apple cider into plastic cups and passed them around.

"Hey, what's this?" Winston asked, wrapping an arm around Elizabeth. "You getting sentimental on us?"

"Just a bit," Elizabeth sniffed, laughing through her tears.

"Here, eat this," Winston offered, handing her a piece of chocolate cake covered with vanilla ice cream. "This will cheer you up."

"Thanks, Winston," Elizabeth said, smiling up at him.

"Here's to the newest reporter for SVU's famous *Chronicle*!" Steven said, holding up his wine glass in the air.

"Hear, hear!" Billie cheered.

Elizabeth sighed as everybody clinked cups. She hadn't told anybody except Jessica about her calamitous last day. And she didn't know how she'd find the courage to tell them. She had made such a big deal about this opportunity, and it turned out to be a total disaster. It was so humiliating. How was she ever going to explain that she just walked out after the second day on the job?

Enid downed her glass. "Oh, Liz, I'm so excited about taking over your 'Personal Profiles' column," she gloated, plopping down next to Elizabeth on the couch. "I already talked to Mr. Collins about it and he said OK."

Elizabeth frowned. Usually Enid wasn't so insensitive. Elizabeth hadn't even officially left yet, and

Enid was already jumping in to take over her life. "I'm really happy for you, Enid," Elizabeth mumbled, lifting her glass to her lips.

"And here's to SVU's latest and greatest cheerleader!" Winston added, holding his glass in the air.

"Oh, Jessica," Lila called across the room. "Heather sent you a message. She wanted to wish you well and let you know how truly pleased she was to be the sole captain of the cheerleading squad."

Jessica glowered. "I bet she's pleased," she said. "Well, that's ridiculous, anyway," she scoffed. "You can't only have one captain on a cheerleading squad. It's too much work for one person. Heather won't be able to choreograph the cheers by herself and lead all the practices, too."

"Jess, do you think I could take your spot?" Amy breathed. "I've always wanted to be cocaptain."

Jessica's brow crinkled into a frown. "Uh, sure, Amy, I guess."

"You're beyond all that amateur high school stuff, anyway," Amy said.

"Yeah, you're really in the big leagues now," Cheryl chorused.

Billie put on Jessica's favorite party tape, and the gang began chattering excitedly about all the high school activities that Jessica and Elizabeth were leaving behind.

As Elizabeth listened, she began to get more and more suspicious. Something was going on. It was possible that her friends would be excited for them, but not this excited. They were up to something, and Elizabeth thought she knew what it was.

Elizabeth glanced over at her twin. Jessica's arms were folded across her chest, and she had a slight smile on her face. Elizabeth caught her eye, and Jessica winked.

"Let's hope this is reverse psychology," Jessica whispered in Elizabeth's ear.

Elizabeth nodded, a smile spreading across her face. "It's a classic case," she whispered back.

"Todd!" Jessica and Elizabeth exclaimed at the same time as Todd walked in the front door, his arms full of chips and soda from the minimart.

Jessica looked around wildly. "Where's Ken?" she asked nervously.

"He's out by the car," Todd said, dumping his bags on the table. "And if you want to catch him, you'd better hurry."

But Jessica was already flying down the hall. She flung open the door and raced down the two flights of steps of the apartment complex. She could hear the motor of Todd's BMW roar to life as she ran across the yard. *Oh no!* she thought as the headlights flashed on and the car backed out of the parking lot and began heading down the street.

Jessica flipped off her heels and grabbed them in one hand, chasing after the car. Now that Ken was so close, she couldn't let him get away. "Ken!" she yelled, waving her arms wildly and running down the street in her stockinged feet. "Wait!"

Ken caught sight of her in the rearview mirror

and pulled over to the side of the road, slowing down to a stop.

Jessica ran around to the passenger side, trying to catch her breath as Ken rolled down the window.

She leaned into the window, resting her elbows on the windowpane. "Ken, we've got to talk," she said, panting rapidly. Her cheeks were flushed pink from exertion.

"Jessica," Ken said, his blue eyes clouded over with hurt, "I don't think we have anything to talk about."

"But Ken, please listen to me," Jessica begged. "You've got to give me a chance to—"

Ken cut her off. "I think you've said quite enough," he said coldly. "Now would you mind getting away from the window?" Ken turned the key in the engine and put his foot on the accelerator.

Jessica quickly opened the car door and climbed in the passenger side before he could get away. He could drive the car away, but she knew he wouldn't kick her out of it. "Please, just hear me out, OK?" Jessica's heart hammered in her chest. She was about to tell Ken the truth, and she didn't know if he would accept it.

Ken shut off the ignition and leaned back in the driver's seat, his arms crossed over his broad chest. Jessica brought her knees up to her chest, warming her feet with her hands.

"Hey, you're barefoot," Ken said softly, leaning over and turning on the heat. Then his face clouded over and became impassive again. Jessica looked down. Ken could be so sweet.

"Ken, I . . . I want to explain," Jessica began in a trembling voice.

Ken held up a hand. "Look, I don't want to hear any more stories," he said. "If you want to talk, I want to hear the truth."

Jessica gulped and nodded. She took a deep breath and gathered her courage. "Well, I started dating this guy named Zach while I was here," she said.

"I noticed," Ken said, closing his eyes and turning away from her.

Jessica swallowed hard. "I think it has something to do with the whole SAT thing. You know how upset I was about it. I felt hurt that you didn't believe I was capable of getting such high scores on my own. I think I was attracted to Zach because he thought I was really smart. He made me feel attractive and intelligent."

"Jessica, I thought we resolved all that," Ken said. "You know I appreciate all of you. And I did support you in the end. I was just a little intimidated. After all, it's not easy to have a girlfriend who's incredibly sexy *and* incredibly smart."

"Well, maybe I was still mad about it," Jessica replied.

Ken looked unconvinced. "There must be more to it than that," he said.

Jessica nodded. Ken was right. That wasn't the whole story. Now she knew why she avoided telling the truth. Because it was awful.

"Well, I guess I thought it would be exciting to

date an older guy," Jessica ventured, looking at Ken nervously.

Ken recoiled as if he had been slapped. "What's wrong, Jess?" he bit out, taking a ragged breath. "High school guys not good enough for you anymore?"

Jessica reddened. "Actually, Zach's in high school, too. I thought he was in college, but it turned out that he's only a high school junior."

"So that's it," Ken said, a muscle twitching angrily in his cheek. "You find out he's not a big frat guy and you decide you want your little high school boyfriend back." Ken clenched his jaw and turned the key in the ignition. "Well, you can forget it, Jessica. I'm not some kind of toy you can play with until a better model comes along." Ken turned toward her, his eyes hard and his face devoid of expression. "Would you mind getting out of the car now?"

"Ken, that's not why I want you back," Jessica explained, tears cascading down her cheeks. Her voice was barely a whisper. "It didn't work out with Zach. The whole time I was with him, I was thinking of you. I couldn't get you out of my mind." Jessica turned imploring eyes to Ken. "Ken, please. I'm telling you the truth now." Jessica almost choked on the words. "You've got to believe me."

Ken's expression had softened. He reached out and ran a finger down her cheek. "I believe you, Jess," he said, his voice hoarse.

Jessica smiled gratefully, the tension easing out of her body. She wiped her eyes with the back of her sleeve. "I realized tonight that you were the one I wanted to be with. I know there's no excuse for my behavior, but maybe I had to learn what I really wanted. The hard way." Jessica reached out and touched his arm. "It's you I love." She looked at him through tear-streaked eyes.

Ken didn't reply. Instead he pulled her gently to him and leaned in to kiss her. Then he kissed her again, softly at first, then with more and more urgency, the kiss deepening until Jessica was lost in it.

After what seemed an eternity, Ken leaned back and smiled at her, his blue eyes tender and full of love.

"Ken?" Jessica asked hesitantly. "Do you forgive me?"

Ken wrapped her up in a hug. "Of course I forgive you," he said. Jessica hugged him back, a tear rolling down her cheek.

"But, Jess, just one thing," Ken said, pulling back to look at her. "The next time you go to Sweet Valley University—?"

"Yes?" Jessica asked.

"I'm coming with you," Ken replied.

"Todd, what was that for?" Elizabeth asked, after she had come up for air. Todd had pulled her into Steven and Billie's bedroom when he arrived, saying they had to talk. And as soon as they had gotten through the door, he had tackled her onto the duvet and began kissing her madly.

"Because I love you," Todd answered, leaning back to gaze into her face.

"I love you, too," Elizabeth said, hot tears pricking

her eyelids. It felt so good to be with Todd again. She hadn't realized how much she'd missed him until this very moment.

"And I've *never* seen you look so sexy," Todd whispered, his warm brown eyes twinkling. "Jessica!" He nibbled at her left shoulder.

"You know!" Elizabeth exclaimed.

"Actually, I have no idea what's going on," Todd said. "But I do know one thing. There's no way you would be seen in public in this getup on your own. And there's no way that Jessica would wear that ball gown. So I figured something was going on. And I assume it has to do with one of Jessica's schemes."

"You're right about that," Elizabeth said. She gave Todd a quick update of the week's events, outlining Jessica's entire scheme in detail.

By the time she was finished, Todd looked thoroughly confused. "So, let me get this straight. You were posing as Jessica with your date, and Jessica was going as Jessica with her date."

"Exactly," Elizabeth said, nodding.

"But . . . but that makes two Jessicas," Todd protested.

Elizabeth nodded again. "One too many, if you ask me."

Todd looked even more perplexed. "But, Liz, isn't there something illogical in that? I mean, isn't the purpose of a twin switch to pretend to be each other?" He scratched his head. "How could there be two of you? Who would that fool?"

"Magda," Elizabeth said with a laugh. "Jessica was

only pretending to be me to Magda. She was still being herself with Zach."

Todd put his head in his hands. "It's too complicated for me," he said. "I can't work it out."

"Well, I guess it worked itself out," Elizabeth replied. "The most important thing is that there's only one Jessica."

"And only one Elizabeth," Todd said softly, cupping her chin in his hand and drawing her toward him for a tender kiss.

"Well, I guess honesty works, huh?" Elizabeth said, looking at her sister's glowing face. Jessica and Ken had walked through the door hand in hand, both of them radiant. Elizabeth had made a beeline for Jessica and dragged her into the kitchen for a sisterly powwow.

"What do you mean?" Jessica asked, turning innocent eyes to Elizabeth. "I told Ken that we were at the Zeta formal on a rush gag. . . ."

Elizabeth's mouth dropped open. "You didn't!" she breathed in horror.

Jessica laughed. "No, I didn't," she said. "Don't worry. I told him the whole truth." She grimaced. "Because you forced me to."

"So did you learn something?" Elizabeth asked.

"Oh, Liz, you are so pedantic," Jessica sighed. "Yes, I learned something. I learned that I can't count on my twin sister when I'm in a bind."

Elizabeth rolled her eyes. "So you worked everything out?" she asked.

Jessica nodded happily. "Yeah, I think Ken has forgiven me," she said. "And I see everything's peachy with you and Mr. Blah Blah."

Elizabeth ignored Jessica's appellation. "Todd was really great about everything," she said, a wistful expression on her face. "You know, I'm really going to miss him."

"Yeah, a long-distance relationship is going to be really hard," Jessica said. "It'll be like saying good-bye all over again every weekend."

Elizabeth sighed and rested her head in her chin. "Now I'm not so sure why we're staying here. College doesn't seem so great anymore now that I've messed up my internship and blown my chance to work with Professor Newkirk."

"Yeah, I know what you mean," Jessica agreed. "I won't be able to try out for the cheerleading squad until next year. I don't know what I'll do with myself."

They both slumped down at the table, staring into space dejectedly.

Suddenly they both sat up. Elizabeth looked at Jessica. "Are you thinking what I'm thinking?"

Jessica nodded, a big smile spreading across her face. "We're going back to Sweet Valley High," she sang.

"Tomorrow," Elizabeth added.

"Tomorrow," Jessica agreed.

"With a little luck, I can get my 'Personal Profiles' column back," Elizabeth said.

"And I can get my cheerleading squad back from Heather," Jessica said.

"Well, should we go tell everybody that their

reverse psychology worked?" Elizabeth asked.

Jessica shook her head. "Let's let them sweat it out for an hour or so," she said with a wicked grin. "After all, we wouldn't want this lavish attention to go to waste!"

Elizabeth rolled her eyes, but couldn't resist a smile. Whether they were at Sweet Valley High, Sweet Valley University, or on the moon, Jessica would always be Jessica!

Has Margo, the Evil Twin, come back to terrorize Jessica and Elizabeth? Don't miss the next Sweet Valley High Magna Edition, **Return of the Evil Twin***, when Margo's own twin, Nora, wants revenge for the death of her sister—and she's capable of evil beyond anything Margo could have ever dreamed!*

Bantam Books in the Sweet Valley High series
Ask your bookseller for the books you have missed

#1	DOUBLE LOVE	#42	CAUGHT IN THE MIDDLE
#2	SECRETS	#43	HARD CHOICES
#3	PLAYING WITH FIRE	#44	PRETENSES
#4	POWER PLAY	#45	FAMILY SECRETS
#5	ALL NIGHT LONG	#46	DECISIONS
#6	DANGEROUS LOVE	#47	TROUBLEMAKER
#7	DEAR SISTER	#48	SLAM BOOK FEVER
#8	HEARTBREAKER	#49	PLAYING FOR KEEPS
#9	RACING HEARTS	#50	OUT OF REACH
#10	WRONG KIND OF GIRL	#51	AGAINST THE ODDS
#11	TOO GOOD TO BE TRUE	#52	WHITE LIES
#12	WHEN LOVE DIES	#53	SECOND CHANCE
#13	KIDNAPPED!	#54	TWO-BOY WEEKEND
#14	DECEPTIONS	#55	PERFECT SHOT
#15	PROMISES	#56	LOST AT SEA
#16	RAGS TO RICHES	#57	TEACHER CRUSH
#17	LOVE LETTERS	#58	BROKENHEARTED
#18	HEAD OVER HEELS	#59	IN LOVE AGAIN
#19	SHOWDOWN	#60	THAT FATAL NIGHT
#20	CRASH LANDING!	#61	BOY TROUBLE
#21	RUNAWAY	#62	WHO'S WHO?
#22	TOO MUCH IN LOVE	#63	THE NEW ELIZABETH
#23	SAY GOODBYE	#64	THE GHOST OF TRICIA
#24	MEMORIES		MARTIN
#25	NOWHERE TO RUN	#65	TROUBLE AT HOME
#26	HOSTAGE	#66	WHO'S TO BLAME?
#27	LOVESTRUCK	#67	THE PARENT PLOT
#28	ALONE IN THE CROWD	#68	THE LOVE BET
#29	BITTER RIVALS	#69	FRIEND AGAINST FRIEND
#30	JEALOUS LIES	#70	MS. QUARTERBACK
#31	TAKING SIDES	#71	STARRING JESSICA!
#32	THE NEW JESSICA	#72	ROCK STAR'S GIRL
#33	STARTING OVER	#73	REGINA'S LEGACY
#34	FORBIDDEN LOVE	#74	THE PERFECT GIRL
#35	OUT OF CONTROL	#75	AMY'S TRUE LOVE
#36	LAST CHANCE	#76	MISS TEEN SWEET VALLEY
#37	RUMORS	#77	CHEATING TO WIN
#38	LEAVING HOME	#78	THE DATING GAME
#39	SECRET ADMIRER	#79	THE LONG-LOST BROTHER
#40	ON THE EDGE	#80	THE GIRL THEY BOTH LOVED
	OUTCAST	#81	ROSA'S LIE

#82 KIDNAPPED BY THE CULT!
#83 STEVEN'S BRIDE
#84 THE STOLEN DIARY
#85 SOAP STAR
#86 JESSICA AGAINST BRUCE
#87 MY BEST FRIEND'S BOYFRIEND
#88 LOVE LETTERS FOR SALE
#89 ELIZABETH BETRAYED
#90 DON'T GO HOME WITH JOHN
#91 IN LOVE WITH A PRINCE
#92 SHE'S NOT WHAT SHE SEEMS
#93 STEPSISTERS
#94 ARE WE IN LOVE?
#95 THE MORNING AFTER
#96 THE ARREST
#97 THE VERDICT
#98 THE WEDDING
#99 BEWARE THE BABY-SITTER
#100 THE EVIL TWIN (MAGNA)
#101 THE BOYFRIEND WAR
#102 ALMOST MARRIED

#103 OPERATION LOVE MATCH
#104 LOVE AND DEATH IN LONDON
#105 A DATE WITH A WEREWOLF
#106 BEWARE THE WOLFMAN (SUPER THRILLER)
#107 JESSICA'S SECRET LOVE
#108 LEFT AT THE ALTAR
#109 DOUBLE-CROSSED
#110 DEATH THREAT
#111 A DEADLY CHRISTMAS (SUPER THRILLER)
#112 JESSICA QUITS THE SQUAD
#113 THE POM-POM WARS
#114 "V" FOR VICTORY
#115 THE TREASURE OF DEATH VALLEY
#116 NIGHTMARE IN DEATH VALLEY
#117 JESSICA THE GENIUS
#118 COLLEGE WEEKEND
#119 JESSICA'S OLDER GUY

SUPER EDITIONS:
    PERFECT SUMMER
    SPECIAL CHRISTMAS
    SPRING BREAK
    MALIBU SUMMER
    WINTER CARNIVAL
    SPRING FEVER

SUPER THRILLERS:
    DOUBLE JEOPARDY
    ON THE RUN
    NO PLACE TO HIDE
    DEADLY SUMMER
    MURDER ON THE LINE
    BEWARE THE WOLFMAN
    A DEADLY CHRISTMAS
    MURDER IN PARADISE
    A STRANGER IN THE HOUSE
    A KILLER ON BOARD

SUPER STARS:
    LILA'S STORY
    BRUCE'S STORY
    ENID'S STORY
    OLIVIA'S STORY
    TODD'S STORY

MAGNA EDITIONS:
    THE WAKEFIELDS OF SWEET VALLEY
    THE WAKEFIELD LEGACY: THE UNTOLD STORY
    A NIGHT TO REMEMBER
    THE EVIL TWIN
    ELIZABETH'S SECRET DIARY
    JESSICA'S SECRET DIARY

SIGN UP FOR THE SWEET VALLEY HIGH® FAN CLUB!

Hey, girls! Get all the gossip on Sweet Valley High's® most popular teenagers when you join our fantastic Fan Club! As a member, you'll get all of this really cool stuff:

- Membership Card with your own personal Fan Club ID number
- A Sweet Valley High® Secret Treasure Box
- Sweet Valley High® Stationery
- Official Fan Club Pencil (for secret note writing!)
- Three Bookmarks
- A "Members Only" Door Hanger
- Two Skeins of J. & P. Coats® Embroidery Floss with flower barrette instruction leaflet
- Two editions of *The Oracle* newsletter
- Plus exclusive Sweet Valley High® product offers, special savings, contests, and much more!

Songs from
the Hit TV Series

Featuring:

"Rose Colored
Glasses"

"Lotion"

"Sweet Valley High
Theme"

Available on CD and Cassette
Wherever Music is Sold.

Life after high school gets even *Sweeter!*

Jessica and Elizabeth are now freshmen at Sweet Valley University, where the motto is: Welcome to college — welcome to freedom!

Don't miss any of the books in this fabulous new series.

♥ College Girls #1   0-553-56308-4 $3.50/$4.50 Can.

♥ Love, Lies and
   Jessica Wakefield #2   0-553-56306-8 $3.50/$4.50 Can.

♥ What Your Parents
   Don't Know #3   0-553-56307-6 $3.50/$4.50 Can.

♥ Anything for Love #4   0-553-56311-4 $3.50/$4.50 Can.

♥ A Married Woman #5   0-553-56309-2 $3.50/$4.50 Can.

♥ The Love of Her Life #6   0-553-56310-6 $3.50/$4.50 Can.